OUT OF
THE BLUE

Dedicated to my mother,

whose stories sustain me today.

Thanks to Karen and Kenya for allowing me writing time.

Contents

Perhaps Love

Indra is lying on a bath towel on the sand on Pigeon Island Beach in St. Lucia. She is next to Rasta Dan, watching the sun disappear below the horizon in the far distance. The heat of the day recedes, overpowered by the cool breeze of the approaching night.

She reaches out and touches the Rasta man's hand. "How are you feeling now?" she asks.

"I am not comfortable with this arrangement Indra," he states.

"What's wrong with it?"

"You have a husband."

"I don't love him. I love you."

"What is love?"

She looks away from Rasta Dan to see the Sandals Grande St. Lucian Spa and Beach Resort. They'd spent the last few nights there. Beyond the resort, she sees the Gros Islet bay and seaside village known for its Friday afternoon street festival of music, food, and local culture. In the far distance, the shimmering lights of the Royal St. Lucian flicker over the water of the Reduit Beach.

She turns to look at Rasta Dan. At twenty-one, he is ten years younger than her and thirty years her husband's junior. They had met at Lion's apartment in Grenada. Two lonely hearts looking for company.

"For me, love is everything. I don't need money, a big house, a fancy car, expensive gifts, nor posh holidays. I need to love someone and for someone to love me back." She peels her eyes away from him to look at Pigeon Island National Park. The night before, they'd attended the jazz festival at the historic park. Many years ago, the island had stood by itself in the Caribbean Sea. The government had dumped and filled the causeway with dredged material to create the beach and access road to the island.

At the jazz festival, she'd listened to a song by Kenneth "Babyface" Edmonds. The song confirmed her suspicions of love. Babyface sang a number - usually done with his group Milestone - called *I Care About You.* She realized that love can be a one-sided affair. She preferred to be on the giving end of love and not an unhappy receiver.

"You plan to tell him you are pregnant for me?"

"Why not?"

"You want to make him crazy?"

"He already crazy over me."

"That will send him off to lunacy."

"Let him."

She stands and runs off down the beach. She runs to the end of the beach, then jogs up past Rasta Dan. On her way back, she jumps into the water and swims out to the demarcation line separating the swimmers from the jet-ski operators.

Rasta Dan stands and wades out into the water. She swims back to him. He lifts her out of the water and into the air like a baby, then lowers her lips to his.

"I don't want to lose you," she says, staring deep into his eyes.

"Face the reality."

"I don't have to."

"You are spending his money on me."

"So?"

"So, you ought to care about him."

"I don't have to," she states. "I have never asked him for anything. He is the one who volunteers to spend money on me."

"Let's get back to the hotel," Rasta Dan says. "Our flights are early in the morning."

They get out of the water and walk arm in arm back to the Sandals Grande.

Back on Grand Cayman, Indra is sitting on the lower deck of the Cayman Cabana Restaurant and Bar in George Town, waiting for her husband, Rahim Rasheed, to finish work.

She examines the menu on the board, struggling to choose. The chef takes local family recipes and produces home cooked food with an added touch of imagination and intricacy, putting a fresh, Caymanian spin on the dishes.

She selects grilled swordfish in the chef's sauce and fries with lemonade.

A man in his fifties dressed in shorts, a polo shirt, and flip-flops walks by with a girl in her twenties wearing a short skirt and skimpy top. What is this young girl doing? This man is twice her age, she thinks. She hoped that this was not the way she and her husband appeared to the public.

The live band on the stand is playing Romain Virgo's version of Adele's - *Stay with me*. She dabs her eyes with tissue as they croon "This ain't love it's clear to see, darling stay with me. Stay with me, coz you're all I need." She wonders if Rahim asked the band to play that song for her.

This is his local bar. He works nearby at the Sea Trek Cayman. Sea Trek Cayman operates from a floating platform at Sotos Reef, named after a pioneer in the Cayman diving industry: Bob Soto.

The dive location is over a sand hole. Divers experience living coral heads up to twenty-five feet in height, thousands of tropical fish, turtles, squid, and a pirate ship's anchor.

She knows Rahim loves the natural sub-aqua terrain. He enjoys being near the Cayman Cabana Restaurant and Bar for the atmosphere and the food.

While the waitress is taking away her plate, she sees Rahim coming. She sips her lemonade as he limps towards her, carrying his diving gear in one hand and a first aid kit in the other. He works as the instructor and diving supervisor at the Sea Trek site. The diving requires no scuba diving certificate or training. Small groups of people don specially designed helmets to walk underwater.

Rahim takes them through the orientation stage, explaining the equipment and the safety features of the experience. He provides them with the personalized touch that Sea Trek prides itself with.

"How was your day, darling?" he asks, lowering himself into a chair.

"I am fine, and you?" she asks.

"Great day. We made two full dives."

The waitress comes around and he orders a coke.

"I am ready to go home," Indra mumbles.

"Let's have a drink together."

"Have it in the car."

"All right."

The waitress brings the coke. Rahim pays the bill and they leave the restaurant. She gets behind the wheel and drives away from the restaurant. Rahim sips his coke as they go. They drive to the house in silence.

Indra turns unto the palm tree-lined driveway of the two beachfront houses in Bodden Town. She drives to the main three-bedroom, two-bathroom house and stops.

Rahim is repairing the second house next door to open a seaside restaurant and bar for Indra. He is putting in a new roof, refitting the interior for commercial kitchen appliances, and constructing a deck on the outside for deck chairs and informal dining tables.

Indra enters the door and runs upstairs to the master bedroom, slamming the door behind her.

Rahim follows her. "Why are you behaving like this?" he asks.

She sits on the bed. "I need a time out," she says.

"You had one," he says. "You just came from the jazz festival in St. Lucia."

"Not that kinda time out."

"What kind of time out?"

"At least a year."

"Why?" he asks.

"I need space."

"Are you not happy here?"

"I don't know."

"What about me? Don't you think I will miss you?"

"I want to go back to Grenada."

"You are only thinking about yourself."

"I have decided. I am going, and you cannot stop me."

"And your restaurant?"

"It will be here."

"You believe the restaurant will sit there waiting for you?"

"Let me worry about that. Take care of yourself." She stands, selects a suitcase, goes to the wardrobe, and packs.

"At least let me drop you to the airport."

"No. You will cry at the airport. I will call a taxi."

"Have it your own way," he says, storming out of the room.

She looks out of the bedroom window to see him patrolling the beach in the backyard, stopping to stare at the ocean. He turns to look at the fifteen thousand-square feet property sitting on ninety feet of beachfront.

She sees the white sand beach with its crystal-clear waters and the coral reef one hundred feet offshore. Rahim told her the location has a diverse tropical fish population. He boasts this beach is ideal for fishing, snorkeling, diving, and water sport.

He told her the restaurant will do well. It will become the premier property on the island.

She walks away from the window, shakes the thoughts from her head, and picks up her bags. She is only focusing on the international airport fifteen minutes away.

Wanda picks up Indra from the Maurice Bishop International Airport in Grenada. They drive along the highway toward the city center.

"Where will you be staying?" Wanda asks.

"I am going back to my apartment in Belmont by Lion," Indra says.

Wanda drives through Grand Anse and turns into the Belmont back road. They stand outside Lion's apartment building.

Indra gets out, walks to the building, and knocks on the door. Lion opens the door. They speak for a few minutes. Indra turns and walks to the car.

"Lion rented out your apartment?" Wanda asks.

"Why didn't you tell me?"

"Woman, I didn't know you were coming. You called me from the airport in Grenada for a ride. Also, I have not been by Lion's since you left."

"I didn't know I was coming. I packed and walked."

"What did Rahim say?"

"He cursed."

"Who would not?"

"You taking his side?"

"It's not a matter of sides Indra." Wanda takes her eyes off the road to stare at her friend. "You need to settle down." She looks to the road.

"I am settled down." Indra sticks up her ring finger at Wanda.

"So why are you here? Without your husband?"

"I have my reasons."

"Where will you live?"

"My mother is alive. She would never turn me down."

"Drop you by your mother?"

"Yes."

"Okay." Wanda turns out of the yard and rejoins the back road. She passes through Paddock and onto the Tanteen Roundabout. They drive in silence up the lane, down Marrast Hill, through the Tempe Roundabout, and onto the Grand Etang main road.

As they drive, Wanda steals a glance at Indra before turning back to the road. Indra feels her friend's eyes. She senses what Wanda is thinking.

"I am pregnant, okay?" Indra blurts out. "You happy now?"

"Ask Rahim," Wanda states. "It's not my child."

"Is not his either."

"You let Rasta Dan breed you?"

"It happened."

"For real?"

"Anyway, it done happen already."

"What did Rahim say?"

"I didn't tell him."

"You run away without telling him?"

"Yes."

Wanda goes silent again.

From the peak at the Grand Etang Lake, they descend into Birch Grove and continue toward Baltazar.

"He gives me everything, but I don't love him."

"Do you know what love is?"

"What do you mean?"

"If love hit you on the head would know it's love?"

"I think so."

"I don't think you know what love is."

"Why?"

"I was like you once. I thought I knew what love is. Do you know the wickedest thing that can happen to you?"

"What?"

"You are the one in love. This Rasta does not care about you. The man who loves you and is there for you—well, you claim you do not love him. He is the one who cares. That's the one who loves you. You know what the worst-case scenario is?"

"Stop talking in parables."

"When you wake up out of your stupor and you realize your mistake, the man gone."

"That will never happen. I know who I love and who loves me."

"Don't say I didn't tell you."

Wanda turns off the main road and crosses the bridge, turning left into Mon Longue Road.

At Mon Longue, Wanda parks the car and helps Indra drag her luggage up the muddy incline to her mother's house. They enter the single room ply house through a side door and place the luggage in a corner.

Indra's mother, Dolly, is in the backyard baking bread in a drum pan oven using coconut husks for fuel.

"I need to pee," Wanda says.

Without turning around, Dolly points her to the outside latrine a few feet away from the backyard. Wanda uses the latrine and then dips a pan into the drum of water under the spouting to wash her hands.

"Thank you for bringing her home," Dolly states. "You want bread to go home?"

"Yes," Wanda states. "Indra shares your bread with me all the time. I love it."

Dolly folds some bread in leaf and brown paper and hands it to Wanda.

"Indra, you will call me when you come to the city," Wanda states.

Indra helps Wanda on the slippery slope to the car. At the bottom, they hug, and Wanda gets into the vehicle and drives away.

Wanda is standing at Dolly's vendor's stall on the sidewalk in the city of St. George. She selects a dasheen, two cabbages, and a parcel of fresh seasoning.

"Dolly, how much do I owe you?" she asks.

"Give me ten dollars," Dolly says.

Wanda hands her the money. Dolly secures it in her apron.

"So, you can't pound sense into your girlfriend's head?" Dolly asks.

"She isn't listening," Wanda states.

"Get her to listen."

"Her head hard."

"I can't throw her out. You see, the state of my house. She cannot expect to stay there and grow up a baby."

"I agree."

"Explain to her. Tell her she must call her husband. She must tell him she made a

mistake. Ask him to take her back. She will take your advice."

"Dolly, I can only promise you to try."

"Please try."

"I will let you know what happens."

"Good girl."

Indra is at Lion's house in Belmont. She is sitting in the living room while Lion attends to a pot on the fire in the open-plan kitchen.

"Indra, I am still sorry, I didn't know you were coming back, so I rented out your place," he says.

"That's okay," she says. "I didn't plan to come back."

"As long as you understand."

"I understand."

"So, we cool."

"We cool."

"Anything you want, let me know."

"I want to call Rahim by Skype."

"The computer is there—go ahead," Lion says. "As long as you don't mind me hearing your conversation."

She walks to the computer and sets up the call. "I don't mind."

Within minutes, Rahim is on the screen, grinning at Indra. "How are you doing, baby?" he asks.

"Coping," she says.

"I miss you."

"I have something to tell you."

"Go ahead, baby."

"I am pregnant."

"That is so great."

"You're happy?"

"I am."

"Are you upset with me?"

"No dear. I want us to live together as a family."

"I couldn't tell you."

"When are you coming back?"

"I am thinking about it."

"Stop thinking and come home. We will go to Miami and shop for the baby."

"I will let you know."

"Great news, baby. Come back."

"I will call you again soon."

"Love you."

"Bye." She ends the call to see Wanda standing by the door looking at her.

"You still didn't tell him the truth?"

"I planned to tell him. It couldn't come out."

"How long you plan to play this game with him?"

"Gosh. I will tell him."

"What's going on?" Lion asks.

"She didn't tell you?" Wanda asks.

"No," Lion says.

"She is pregnant for Rasta Dan and she is scared to tell her husband."

"Rasta Dan?" Lion asks. "That ole lazy good-for-nothing wretch."

"Don't judge me guys," Indra says.

"We are your friends," Lion states. "We have a duty to sack it to you as it is."

"I will explain everything to him in due course," Indra says.

"You better do it sooner rather than later," Lion states.

"She claims she loves the Rasta but does not love her husband," Wanda says.

"Indra, you better stop that," Lion states. "You call it love? Using your husband's money to mine a lazy man?"

"I don't expect you to understand."

"Make us understand. We're listening," Lion says.

"I need not explain," Indra states. "I know it's love."

"I am sorry for you," Lion says.

"The food ready?" Indra asks.

"Yes, run away from the problem." Lion smirks. "The food is ready. Take what you want from the pot."

Indra and Wanda go to the pot. They fill a bowl each with dumplings, green bananas, turtle, conch, octopus, fish, and fish waters.

They sit around the dining table to eat. Lion flicks on the television set. The weather report is on, showing the devastation caused by the hurricane in Barbuda.

"Barbuda done," Lion exclaims.

"The whole island mash-up," Wanda says.

"It's moving up towards Puerto Rico, Anguilla, and Tortola at category five," Lion says.

"They better batten down," Wanda states.

Indra finishes eating, then does the dishes in the kitchen sink.

"Wanda, I want a lift to the bus stop," she says.

"Anytime you ready," Wanda states.

"Indra, you don't look concerned about the hurricane," Lion says.

"No. I don't know anybody in those places." She completes the dishes, says goodbye to Lion, and leaves with Wanda.

Two days later, Indra returns to Lion's house to call Rahim on Skype. Lion is in the kitchen cooking while Wanda sits on the couch, watching the hurricane destroy Miami.

"You guys are right," she says. "I need to level with Rahim. I owe him that."

Wanda and Lion look at her. "What made you come to your senses?" Lion asks.

"I can't live at my mother's house anymore," she says. "I cannot grow up a baby under those conditions."

"Isn't that how you grew up?" Wanda asks.

"That was then, this is now," she states.

She walks to the computer and calls. A strange woman is on the screen.

"I want to talk to Rahim," Indra states.

"You are Indra? The woman who dumped him?"

"I am his wife."

"You mean his other wife."

"What do you mean?"

"He has a wife and two children in Tortola."

"I am his only wife."

"That's what you thought."

"Who are you?"

"I am his girlfriend from East End."

"Where is he?"

"He went to Tortola to help his family during the hurricane."

"When is he coming back?"

"He is not coming back."

"He went to live with the woman?"

"No, he died during the hurricane."

"Oh no," she shouts, and shudders.

Wanda and Lion walk over to console her.

THE END

The Fling

Reggie and his lead singer are in the basement of his house practicing for his live show at the all-inclusive hotel that weekend. He picks up the tenor sax and blows to the rhythm of Whitney Houston's song *I Will Always Love You.*

His lead singer cues in and croons to the automated melody filling the room.

She stops, and Reggie blows again, soothing the soundproof room with sweet music. Penny, his wife, enters the studio and listens for a while. She claps.

"You deserve a round of applause," she says. "You deserve a standing ovation." She looks at the lead singer. "You should join in. Give him a round of applause. Congratulations!"

Reggie stops blowing, allowing the sax to hang from the strap around his neck. "What are you doing here?" he asks. "Why are you disturbing my practice?"

"You should join in too," she says. "Give yourself a round of applause."

"What are you doing?"

"Congratulations are in order."

"For what?"

"Your new baby."

"Penny, have you been drinking? Are you losing your mind?"

She turns to the lead singer. "Didn't he tell you he was horning you with a twelve-year-old girl? She's pregnant!"
The lead singer drops the microphone and storms out of the studio.

"Don't go," he shouts.

"You should rot in hell," Penny says, and follows the lead singer out of the studio.

Reggie removes the sax from around his body and places it on a nearby stand. He turns off the music and steps away from the bandstand. At the sidebar, he pours a Scotch on the rocks. Using the side door, he steps out onto the lawn.

The sax player looks around at his manicured lawn and the swimming pool in the middle. He sees the wooden fence on each side leading to the outdoor kitchen, sports bar, and grill at the end.
He strolls along the edge of the saxophone-shaped pool toward the sports bar and turns to face the rear of his house.

At forty-five, he had done well for himself, with the help of Penny. The two-story great house was an old plantation mansion sitting on a hill overlooking the entire estate. They'd bought it five years ago after their honeymoon. It had gone through many modifications, including the pool and the outdoor bar, and they loved the final product.

Their wedding had been huge. Every important family on the island attended. A respected inspector of police marrying a thirty-year-old attorney of law coming from an upper-class family.

Soon after, he'd become an assistant superintendent of police (ASP), while his wife rose in prominence within the legal fraternity. Reggie sips on the Scotch and sits. It is a wonderful life. He wonders if he'd blown it with a foolish fling.

He remembered how he'd met the young lady. Six months earlier, he'd seen her running on the beach. He'd encouraged his lead singer to befriend her and gain her details. Within a week, he'd taken over communication using WhatsApp and had established a direct line to her.

By the next week, he had her running away from home at night while her mother went to work as a nurse at the general hospital. She would slip out of her mother's house to meet him on a side road.

Two weeks ago, she'd told him she was ten weeks pregnant. Her mother forbade her from aborting the baby. He recalls how furious he'd been.

He sips on the Scotch and looks toward the pool. Penny's dachshund poodle wriggles towards him, tongue outstretched, panting and wagging its tail. He kicks it into the swimming pool.

Penny is sitting next to the commissioner of police on the bleachers of the stadium looking at the policemen practice their drills for the upcoming Independence Day parade.

Reggie, dressed in his ASP uniform, is leading the police band at a fast tempo as they go through their routine.

"How long you knew this?" the commissioner asks.

"He has been with this young girl for at least six months," Penny says.

"What do you plan to do?"

"I will divorce him."

"Are you sure?"

"I am sure."

"You don't want to wait? Do a DNA?"

"No, commissioner. This will not happen again."

"He has done it before?"

"More than once."

"What do you expect of me?"

"As much as I love him, he needs help. He is an officer of the law who has no qualms about breaking the law. Can you help him?"

"I don't know."

"You are his boss."

"I wish I was."

"What do you mean?"

"I have a boss."

"Oh my god."

"He is the man."

"Then talk to him."

"I will talk to him."

They look on as the parade marches through its steps. The men and women shift around and march until they form themselves into different letters and shapes before being dismissed. The men shuffle out of the park.

Penny says goodbye to the commissioner and leaves the grounds. The commissioner watches her leave.

"In your younger days, she wouldn't get away," the prime minister says.

The commissioner looks around, shocked. "You were there all the time chief?" he asks.

"No, I snuck up on you," the prime minister says. "You get old. Imagine I could just sneak up on you like that."

"She had me distracted."

"She could distract me anytime."

"Not that way boss." The Commissioner flings his hand.

"Our conversation was disturbing."

"About the underage girl the husband breed?"

"Boss, you have that information?"

"I am the minister of national security. I get everything," the prime minister states.

"She wants us to do something about it."

"We cannot go public. Deal with it."

"But it is a crime?"

"Can you deal with a scandal now?"

"No."

"Neither can I. An election is coming up," the prime minister stresses. "So, do what you have to do."

"Okay boss."

"I am heading home now." The prime minister and his bodyguards leave. People trickle from the stadium. The commissioner sits there.

The commissioner empties a full clip of ammunition into the target. Of the ten rounds from the Glock, five hit the bullseye while five passed through the inner circle. He grins at Reggie.

"Young boy," he says. "Lemme see if you still have it."

Reggie steps up to the line, lifts his earth-toned Beretta, wraps his hand around the customized grip, and empties the full fifteen-round clip into the target. He pulls it back. Six slugs hit the bullseye, four hit the inner circle, while the other five hit around the target.

"I am out of practice," Reggie admits.

"Losing your sharpness, ASP," the commissioner states.

"I must admit," Reggie says.

They continue to shoot at the targets several more times before removing their headgear and gloves.

The men walk to the rear of the commissioner's SUV. The commissioner opens the rear door and lifts the lid of his cooler.

"What's your poison?" he asks.

"I will have a beer," Reggie says.

The commissioner pops open a can of Kronenbourg 1664 and hands it to Reggie. He selects a Guinness and uses an opener to flick open the cap.

"You're not yourself today my boy." The commissioner sips on the Guinness. "Your wife and I spoke."

"Boss, I am confused."

"The PM does not want publicity. He cannot afford a scandal."

"Where does that leave me?"

"I don't know."

"What would you suggest?"

"Run like hell. Before the heat gets worse."

"Will you help me leave?"

"I can't help you." The commissioner sips on his Guinness again. "However, we did not have this conversation. If you were to leave the island, nobody will stop you."

"I understand," Reggie says, drinking the last of his beer. "Thank you so much."

He salutes the commissioner and marches toward his vehicle.

Reggie and twenty-two-year-old Tamara sit at the bar in the kitchen of her apartment in Brooklyn, New York, having breakfast. "Sorry I could not pick you up last night," Tamara says. "Work was busy."

"Got a cab," Reggie states. "We found your address."

"Great," she says. "Remember two years ago? You came to cool out."

"They accused me of ill-discipline and behavior unbecoming of a police officer."

"We had a blast. How long do you plan to stay?"

"About two weeks."

"You are welcome."

"What are you doing today?"

"I am off today. We can go to bed now. Later we will go for a drink." She grins.

"I am down for whatever."

"You're learning the twang, my brother."

"I am a quick learner."

They finish breakfast and head toward the bedroom.

Penny and her sister Jenelle sit in the corner of a restaurant downtown having lunch. They are both having grilled grouper and salad with sauté potatoes. Penny is having orange juice while Jenelle sips on bottled water.

"You think I am acting hastily?" Penny asks.

"Yes."

"This is not his first time."

"So why divorce him this time?"

"There is a slight difference this time." Penny looks Jenelle in the eyes. "He cannot cover up this one."

"I cannot tell you what to do. However, consider divorce carefully. Consider having to start a new life. Finding a new husband. Think about your status in society and your position in the church. There are many issues to think about."

"That's why you didn't divorce your husband when he ran off with the Indian chick?" Penny quips, laughing.

"My situation was different," Jenelle states.

"How?"

"He came back." Jenelle signals to the waiter. "He returned and repented. As a good catholic, I forgave him. He is behaving now."

"So, I should wait?"

"Maybe."

"I don't think he is coming back."

"I suspect so. Allow time to pass. Do not jump to conclusions."

The waiter comes to the table.

"Let us see the dessert menu," Jenelle says.

"I will have an espresso and a shot of Drambuie," Penny states.

"That is a hard act to follow," Jenelle says. "Don't bother with the menu. I will have cheesecake and ice cream."

"What flavor ice cream?"

"One scoop coconut, one scoop cherry vanilla."

"Any toppings?"

"Your choice."

"Coming up," the waiter says. He clears the table and goes to the kitchen.

"I will have to wait for five years to pass before I can file for a no-contest divorce," Penny states.

"That is true," Jenelle says. "Nobody wants to go down the route of a contested divorce where each party gets to wash all their dirty rags in public."

"This conversation is premature."

"Premature but necessary."

"I agree."

The waiter returns with the desserts. The pair enjoy their desserts in silence.

"The dessert is good," Jenelle says.

"Loaded with calories," Penny says.

The waiter comes to the table with the bill. Penny gives him her credit card. He clears the table and walks to the cashier, handing over the credit card. Within minutes he returns to the table.

"Miss, we tried your card three times, but it declined. Do you have another card? Or would you like to pay cash?"

"How could that be?" Penny asks. "This is a debit card. There is money in the account."

Jenelle takes her purse from her handbag and pays the bill in cash. "You can keep the change," she says. "We are sorry for the inconvenience."

"Thank you for coming," the waiter says. "Come again."

Back in Brooklyn, Reggie and Tamara are in the basement of DJ Fowler's bar having a drink with their backs against the bar. A man approaches Reggie. "Ah hear you run from home?" he says. Reggie ignores him.

"They say you not going back? The man insists. Reggie continues to ignore him.

"You breed a twelve-year-old," the man continues. Reggie pushes himself off the bar, takes one step forward, and floors the man with a punch to the side of the jaw.

In one movement, he tosses money on the bar and drags Tamara out of the basement toward the car. They drive in silence, with Tamara staring out of the window most of the way.

They enter the apartment, hang up their jackets, remove their shoes, and walk toward the living room. Tamara jumps at him. She grabs him by the collar and pushes him onto the three-seater couch.

"Tell me what is going on," she demands.

"I don't know," he says.

"How you mean?" she asks.

"I don't," he insists.

"You punched down that guy."

"He had it coming to him. He is always teasing me."

"Was he wrong?"

"Yes. He is a fool."

She eases off him and flops onto the couch. Without hesitation, he covers her with his body. She responds.

Reggie sets out early in the morning to find his long-time friend Bill. He takes the train to Atlantic Avenue, where Bill runs a garage and shipping agency. At the garage, he sees Bill walking around in the yard while talking on his mobile phone. He stands next to a vehicle while Bill wraps up his conversation.

Bill flicks off the cellphone and walks toward Reggie. "Reggie, ma man, good to see you," he says. "Heard you were around."

"Yeah, am here," Reggie responds.

"Come in, ma brother." Bill signals to the trailer office at the corner of the garage. "Let's knock a glass for old times' sake."

Reggie follows him into the trailer.

Bill saunters to the back of his leather chair and opens a cabinet. "Scotch on the rocks good for you?" he asks without turning.

"Perfect," Reggie says.

Bill mixes the drinks and turns to face Reggie. "Have a seat, man," he says, handing Reggie his drink.

Reggie sips on his scotch, recoiling at the impact in his throat.

"Not Buckingham Palace, but it serves the purpose."

Reggie sits and sips on his drink. "Good Scotch," he says.

"Only drink the best," Bill claims. "So, what brings you here, ma man?"

"Ah looking for work."

"That is difficult to come by."

"I am prepared to do anything," Reggie states. "Live music gigs at a bar or a restaurant."

"I will keep my eyes open." Bill sits.

"Fine by me," Reggie says.

"I owe you one anyway," Bill states. "You remember when you arrested me with the quarter-pound of weed?"

"Yes."

"You were a constable."

"Not too long on the force," Reggie says.

"You helped me escape."

"I was sorry for you man."

"I owe you one. It forced me to run to America. I always wondered: what became of the weed?"

Reggie takes another sip of Scotch, twisting in his seat. "They destroyed it," he claims.

"I always wondered."

"Bill, I think I have taken enough of your time. I have a few places to go," Reggie says. "Keep me posted."

"Yes, my brother," Bill confirms. "I will keep you posted."

Reggie finishes his drink and leaves the office. As he walks between the cars in the garage, he sees one of Bill's workers scamper into the office shouting. He listens to the conversation.

"That is Reggie? The ASP?" the worker asks.

"That's the man," Bill says.

"What is he doing here?"

"He is looking for work."

"And he come to you?"

"Yes."

"He dunno how people hate him?"

"He helped me once but only because he wanted to sell the weed for himself."

"So you gonna help him?"

"Help who?"

"The ASP."

"You saw an ASP come here?"

Reggie walks away from the garage.

Jenelle, dressed in her nursing scrubs, her eyes red, marches past Penny's secretary and bursts into her office. She blows her nose into a tissue.

Penny asks her client to excuse the sisters for a short while. Jenelle whips a newspaper from her handbag and flings it onto Penny's desk.

"Reggie is starring in the papers," Jenelle sobs. "They claim they've been following this story for a long time. More details have emerged, allowing them to print it."

Penny picks up the newspaper and reads the article on the front page captioned, *Senior Police Officer on the Run.*

"They have the full story," Penny says.

"They claim he punched a man in New York."

"While hanging out with his foreign woman."

"He also approached people, begging for work."

"Son of a bitch."

"Did you read this part?" Penny looks up from the newspaper. "They claim he sent in his resignation to the Public Service Commission."

"Did he discuss that with you?"

"He has not been in touch since he left." Penny is shuddering.

"He is appalling."

"I have no choice now," Penny sobs. "I must file for divorce."

"Agreed."

"Let me put the papers in motion."

"Please hurry. You have my full support now."

Penny walks around her huge mahogany desk and hugs her sister. "Thank you for being there for me sis," she says.

"You can count on me," Jenelle states. "I will always be your support. It is his loss. He is losing a solid woman."

The women compose themselves, dry their eyes, and Jenelle says goodbye.

Penny leans out of the door and asks her client to return.

Reggie returns to Tamara's doorstep to find his suitcase on the porch and a copy of the newspaper on top of it. He turns his key in the lock, but it does not work. He knocks on the door.

Tamara opens the door dressed in a robe and clutching a box of soft tissues.

"Thought you were at work?" he asks.

"I didn't go," she says.

"Why is my suitcase outside?"

"Because you are leaving."

"Where am I going?"

"I don't care," she sobs, dabbing her eyes with tissue. "You return to my life full of lies. I have protected myself from people like you. I have maintained my sanity. You left me to marry into money after abusing me for all those years. Yet I dreamed of your return. Here you are at last. Now this." She points at the newspaper.

"But baby…"

"There is no "but baby". I have been there. This young girl is me. I was thirteen when you forced me to abort my baby." She slams the door.

THE END

Robbie-Ann

Robbie-Ann tiptoes past her six sisters sleeping on the floor and climbs out through the window of the plywood house. She lands four feet below in the yard. She sneaks around to the back of the house and into the banana and bluggoe trees, retrieving the backpack she'd stashed there earlier.

Her mother, Doreen, hears her and opens her eyes. She listens to the shuffling and rustling and looks at the time on her cellphone. 1:00 a.m. She closes her eyes again trying to fall back to sleep.

On the mattress next to her, her husband, Underpants, lies asleep, snoring like a juggernaut. Doreen murmurs a silent prayer. Robbie-Ann slides between the trees and breaks into a run when the vegetation gives way to a track leading to the main road. At the main road, she catches her breath and waits to thumb a lift.

Several vehicles pass her by before she walks south. As she walks, a car pulls up and the driver leans over to offer her a lift. She accepts and enters the rear seat of the car.

"Miss, please come to the front seat," the driver says. "I am not running a taxi tonight and I sure you have no money to pay for this ride."

She continues to sit in the rear of the car. The driver moves off, muttering to himself. He drives on for a mile in silence.

"What is your name?" he asks.

She sits in the rear of the car and does not answer.

They drive for another two miles.

"Where are you going?" the driver asks.

Robbie-Ann maintains her silence.

The driver stops. "You know what." He turns around and bares his teeth at her. "I can do without this crap. Get out of my car."

She climbs out of the car and continues walking. The driver moves away.

Within minutes, he stops the car and reverses. He stops next to her. "Look, young lady, just take the ride," he says. "You don't have to talk to me."

She ignores him and keeps on walking.

He drives away again.

Robbie-Ann walks up a driveway, passing a minibus and a sports car in the yard. She knocks on the front door. A woman dressed in a jogging suit opens the door.

"Yes?" the woman says.

"I come to Surewine," Robbie-Ann says.

The woman looks at her Fitbit. "At five in the morning?"

"Yes."

If you say so. Wait here." The woman disappears into the house.

A lanky greying man in his fifties comes walking out in his nightclothes. He steps outside and pulls the door behind him.

"What the hell you doing here?" he asks. "You going off?"

"I have nowhere else to go."

"What am I going to tell Mary?"

"Tell her I am your niece."

The woman in the jogging suit opens the door and steps out. "What's going on Surewine?" she asks. "Who is this?"

"This is my niece."

"You niece? I don't know this one."

"Is an outside child me brother have."

"Handle your business. I am going for a run." The woman runs along the driveway.

Robbie-Ann watches Mary disappear around the corner then turns her attention back to Surewine. He holds her hand and leads her into the house. They move along a corridor and into a bedroom.

"We have an hour before she come back," he says, stripping off his tee-shirt. "We can do something quick."

She drops her backpack and lies on the bed.

Surewine is sitting at the table in the dining room, dressed in a polo shirt and jeans. He is having coffee, orange juice, bacon, eggs, and toast for breakfast when Mary returns.

"Where is the girl?" she asks.

"I gave her a room," he says.

"For how long?"

"Just for the day. She fell asleep. She had a hard night."

"Then she goes home."

"Yes."

"I am working a little late today. You should grab something for your dinner on the outside."

"And you. What will you have?"

"I will be all right. I will have lunch from the canteen and a hot drink for dinner."

Surewine finishes his breakfast and goes to the toilet to clean up.

Mary sneaks into the hallway, opens the bedroom door, and looks at the sleeping girl. She closes the door and walks back to the foot of the stairs to the master bedroom. Surewine comes out of the toilet, kisses her on the lips, drags on his sneakers, walks out of the door, and steps into the bus. He cranks the engine and drives out of the yard.

Mary climbs the stairs to the master bedroom. Within minutes, she is downstairs again dressed in her inspector of police uniform. She heads for the door. She exits, climbs into the sports car, and leaves the yard.

A police sergeant and a constable are standing in front of Robbie-Ann's house, questioning her father and mother.

"So, Underpants. Or should I call you Mr. Underpants?" the sergeant asks.

"You know everybody calls me Underpants," the father says.

"You woke up this morning and she was gone. That is your statement."

"That's right."

"Miss. Doreen, you confirm that?" he turns to the mother.

"Yeah," she says, bowing her head to fiddle with her dress. The sergeant follows her gaze. "You pregnant again, Miss Doreen?" She nods her head in the affirmative.

"Underpants, you doesn't sleep?" the sergeant says.

"She want the boy." Underpants grins.

"You can't mine what you have. You making more?"

"The Lord will provide," Doreen mutters.

"As you know, we cannot report her missing until she has been gone for forty-eight hours," the sergeant states. "When I get to the station, I will send around an internal notice. I will ask officers nationwide to look out for her. I cannot send out a missing person's bulletin yet."

"Thank you, officer," the father states.

"Just to confirm" - the sergeant flips his notebook - "she is fourteen years old, five feet four inches tall, and weighs one hundred and ten pounds. A scar on her forehead. Dress unknown, hairstyle unknown."

"Yes," the father confirms.

"Do you know why she ran away from home?"

"No," the father says.

"Miss Doreen?"

"No," she says, staring at the ground.

"Well, that's it for now," the sergeant states. "Do have a nice day."

"Thank you, officer," Underpants says.

The private walks to the police van and climbs behind the wheel. The sergeant climbs into the passenger seat.

"What a mess," he says.

"Seven children in a one-bedroom ply house and still making more."

"She says the Lord would provide."

"I hope she knows the Lord only helps those who help themselves."

"You know your Bible, private." The sergeant laughs.

"Don't ask me which verse?" He turns the vehicle around and begins to descend the muddy track leading from the house.

"Didn't you get the feeling she is hiding something?" the sergeant asks.

"Yeah, Sarge."

"Give them time," the sergeant states. "We will soon see."

Underpants puts on a pair of dirty overalls, damp socks, and water-resistant rubber boots before slinging his weed-eater over his shoulder and leaving the house. He walks for four hundred meters to meet his road gang of workers.

The gang comprises five people tasked with cleaning the roadside: four women and a man with a weed-eater. It is an irregular job. The government assembles these gangs three or four times per year to do the work.

He joins the waiting women, cranks his weed-eater into action and cuts the grass. After ten minutes, he allows the women to clean up and dispose of the trash. One woman moves within his earshot and gathers the loose grass. "Ah hear you daughter run away again boy," she says for everyone to hear.

He glares at her and remains silent.

"You know she have a busman?" another asks.

He grunts, walks away from the women, and heads to the shop across the road. He orders a strong rum and water. The barman serves him.

"Wha' you looking at?" he barks at the barman.

"Miss me yes mister, I have nothing to say to you," the barman replies.

He pulls out coins from his pocket and slaps them on the table. "This is my money ah spending."

"My taxpayers' money," the barman retorts, picking up the coins and counting them.

"Ah wuk for it."

"Ten minutes work? With a machine? You call that work?"

"Ah going back to wuk." He tosses the strong rum into the back of his throat, swallows the water, and leaves the shop.

He walks away from the women, cranks the weed-eater into action, and attacks the grass.

Mary is sitting in her office entering logs on the computer when her secretary sticks her head through the open door.

"The chief wants to see you," she says.

Mary saves her work and stands. "Did he say what it is?"
"No."

She leaves her office and walks up the stairs to the commissioner of police's office. She enters the door and approaches the secretary.

"Wait a minute," the secretary says. "He is just finishing up something."

Within minutes, the commissioner's door opens and a private comes out with her uniform disheveled.

"Come here young lady," Mary says. "You cannot go out there with your uniform in disarray like that." She fixes the young lady's uniform and straightens her belt. "Now, that is better."

The young private scuttles out of the office.

"Thank you, Inspector," the commissioner booms from his doorway. "You have to keep teaching them a thing or two these days."

Mary walks into the office and remains standing.

"Sit down, darling," the commissioner says.

"Commissioner," she whispers as she sits on the chair, pointing to his open fly.

The commissioner zips up his fly and sits in his high-backed chair. He pulls out a small file from his top right-hand drawer and extracts a picture from it.

"Do you recognize this girl?"

"Yes, that is Surewine's niece."

"Niece," the commissioner shouts. "That is the kinda crap he feeds you with." He passes another picture from the file to Mary. She studies the picture for a while. "Can I take a shot of this?"

"Go ahead. Have a feast." The commissioner sniggers. "I have more. Do you want to see the others?"

"This is enough for me."

"The special branch took these."

"You had him followed?"

"They were monitoring a drug-related matter. They came upon this by accident."

"What should I do?"

"Leave him. Come back to me. Ah still ha sugar for you."

"You forget you married?"

"Me wife doh digging nuttin."

"That is impossible. You married her over me. I cannot forget that. Just sweep it under the carpet."

"That is old history. You must learn to let go."

"I am not coming back to you. I was young and vulnerable, just leaving school and entering the police service. You took advantage of my innocence."

"What will you do?"

"I will confront him when I go home. I want to hear what he says."

"You sure you don't want to see the other photos? They are graphic. The boys feasted their eyes."

"No. I can do without that. You and the boys have fun."

"I wish you luck."

"Thanks." Mary stands, salutes the commissioner, and leaves the office.

After his last trip at five in the afternoon, Surewine abandons the bus route and heads for home. He meets Robbie-Ann on the couch. She is in the living room, eating crackers and cheese and drinking juice. She is wearing one of his basketball tee-shirts.

He sits next to her. "How was your day?"

"I feel good," she says, smiling. "I woke up around two, had a bath, borrowed your jersey, read a book, and came here to watch a little tv."

"I'm pleased." He cuddles her and kisses her on the lips.
She smiles and snuggles up to him.

"You know this would not last," he warns. "You will have to go home."

"I am not going back home."

"You cannot stay here."

"I am not going back."

"What do you want me to do?"

"Your wife thinks I am your niece. She does not know about us."

"We will see how that goes."

"I wouldn't say anything."

"Anyway, we have an hour before she gets home." He stands and leads her to the bedroom across the hallway.

Surewine jumps up from the bed as the car pulls into the yard. Robbie-Ann is sound asleep under the covers. He drags on his pants, grabs his shirt, sprints to the kitchen, and flicks on the kettle. He is sitting at the bar in the kitchen with a cup and a tea bag when his wife arrives.

"Where is the girl?" she asks.

"She is in the room."

"Did you speak to her?" she asks. "Did she tell you why she left home?"

"Nah. I didn't have the time to speak to her."

"Make me a cup of tea," she says, "I must get out of this uniform. I will be back to join you for tea."

"That would be nice." He smiles.

She leaves the kitchen and goes toward the stairs to the master bedroom. When she returns to the kitchen, Surewine has the cup of tea and a plate of crackers and assorted cheeses waiting for her. She takes a sip of tea and pops a cracker with cheese into her mouth. She whips out her phone, pulls up the picture from the commissioner's office, and shows it to Surewine.

"You and your niece engaged in a kiss."

"I was congratulating her on something," he claims. "I gave her a kiss. What is wrong with that?"

She measures him. "Do you know who took this picture?"

"No."

"The special branch," she measured him more. "You want me to show you the rest of them?"

"Okay," he concedes. "I will drop her home in the morning."

"Not in the morning. She is going home tonight," Mary states. "I am calling one of my officers to take her home."

She retrieves her phone and dials a number.

The next morning, Underpants comes home from his roadwork before lunchtime. He sits on the wooden step to remove his waterproof boots and socks before entering the house.

He sees Robbie-Ann folded in a corner, sweating and shivering in the heat, muttering words to herself.

"Thought you could run forever," he grumbles.

She glances at him and continues to shake. Her mutterings become louder but stay incomprehensible.

He drops his overall to stand naked in front of her. She tries to scream, but he covers her mouth with his huge dirty hands.

Doreen is in the sink under the house washing clothes. She pauses for a while to listen to the sounds coming through the plywood flooring. She mops her forehead with a rag and continues washing.

In the afternoon, Robbie-Ann is sitting by the river, foaming and frothing from her mouth. She is clutching a bottle in her hand as she falls to the ground. She crawls along the river's bank to the edge of the water and drinks.

Her grip on the bottle loosens. It floats away into the stream, spinning and tossing, the skull and bones hazard label flashing with each spin.

THE END

The Offshore Banker

They say we took in over five hundred million United States dollars at Singular Bank, my offshore bank on the island of Sokas. We did not. At most, we reached three hundred million dollars.

The day they booted me out of Sokas began with a summons to the prime minister's house.

I got myself together and hopped outside. My driver had the engine running. I dragged myself into the car and secured my crutches across the seat. I held a brown envelope in my hand, which rested on my lap.

We travelled from the villa I'd bought in the south, passing along the coastal road, bypassing the city center, and heading uphill toward the prime minister's official residence. We entered a wooded expanse, a rainforest, within the town's perimeter. As I looked out of the car's window, the trees slid backwards.

We climbed further into the hills until the trees gave way to a wide-open yard. The house sat in the middle, with a tennis court off to one side. Four hundred meters beyond the house, the president's majestic house was visible.

The driver pulled into the yard and I stepped out, manipulating the crutches to steady myself. I'd lived on the island long enough to know that when the prime minister summoned you to his house, you went.

I climbed to the top of the stairs, leading with my left leg and dragging the right. At the top of the stairs, I entered the verandah. I held onto the rail to steady myself and catch my breath. I was still struggling for breath when the prime minister stepped out of the house to meet me. He surveyed me then turned toward an open door at one end of the verandah.

"Follow me," he grunted. I followed him into his home office. "You brought the thing?"

"Yes, Prime Minister," I said handing him the brown envelope I carried in my hand. He tossed the envelope onto his desk without opening it.

"Why didn't you send it through the normal channel yesterday?"

"I knew I was coming here soon," I stuttered. "Thought I would bring it myself. I added a little for appreciation."

He frowned and looked straight through me. "Sit down."

I did.

He sat behind his huge mahogany table and slapped the wood. "Made by prisoners. From good old local mahogany," he said. "These days, world human rights organizations are saying you cannot do this anymore. You cannot violate the human rights of the prisoners. They must not work. This is how the world operates. As soon as some government or international organization kicks up against anything, we as small countries have to stop doing it."

I moved to answer, but he waved his hand.

"The British and the Americans insist that I must get rid of you and your offshore bank." He glanced at the envelope. "I have no choice."

"Prime Minister, this is impossible," I protested, staring at the envelope. "We have a good thing going."

"Don't you think I know?" he asked.

"Why don't you resist them?"

"You have forty-eight hours." He stood and signaled to the door.

"Are you referring to my entire operation? The Singular Growth Fund *and* the Singular Exchange, or just Singular Bank?"

"The entire operation." The prime minister grinned. "You are the CEO of all of them, aren't you?"

"Yes, I am."

"There are no exceptions," he said.

The number of security guards had increased. One was now standing by the exit door of the home office, another at the entrance. Beyond him I noticed another strolling in the verandah.

"Goodbye Prime Minister," I muttered while heading for the door. Out of the corner of my eye, I saw him open the envelope to count the money.

Navigating the stairs was more difficult than it had been coming up, but I made it to the waiting car and climbed into the backseat, dragging the crutches with me. We sped out of the yard.

"The office," I said.

I settled back in the seat and pulled the handset from its cradle between the front seats and dialed Tom Barclay. Tom was the bank's attorney at law and my director of operations.

"Tom, how are you doing?" I asked.

"It's a great day, Dan," He said. "How did your meeting go?"

"We have forty-eight hours to shut down operations and leave."

"That's impossible."

"My sentiments."

"Did you tell him about the eight hundred million we are working on?"

"He was not listening."

"We need to tell somebody."

"That's your job."

"I will," he said. "I will keep you informed on my progress."

"Good man. Have a great day," I said, replacing the handset.

Tom came well-recommended. He was a member of the Inner Temple in London, where he had done pupilage. He'd attended Cambridge University, getting a first degree in Accounting and Finance before switching to Law. At forty-two, he had completed an LLM in International Law and was on the short list to become a Queen's Counsel.

Over the past four years, he'd become more than a legal adviser. We were friends. He ran the day-to-day operations of the bank and its related entities. If anyone could find a way through the next forty-eight hours, it was Tom.

The driver pulled into the bank's car park and I struggled and wobbled into my office through the side entrance and crashed into my chair. Toni Spelling, my trusted administrative assistant, heard me come in.

"Dan, you're sneaking into your own office now?" she asked as she swung her hips and smiled at me as I sat helpless in the chair. "When are you going to get that hip replacement?"

"Which one do you think is more urgent?" I asked without looking at her. "My hip or my heart?"

"You decide."

"Did I tell you that I have half a liver and only one kidney?"

"No."

"So much I did not tell you."

"When are you going to tell me?"

"Not now. Get me some coffee," I snapped at her.

"It's on the way," she said. "Anything else?"

"Get me the file on the Omanbutu Foundation," I snapped again.

Toni turned and headed for the door. She stopped and looked at me. I glared at her.

Toni was a good girl. I'd met her within days of arriving on the island. The chemistry was there; we were two lost souls looking for new exploits. I'd been trying to settle into island life and get my bank established, while Toni had been looking for stability and funds to finance her lavish lifestyle. She had outgrown the supportive abilities of the local men.

My money made her a woman. She traveled to Miami for training three times per year. The training and international exposure transformed her. She became my administrative assistant and human resource manager and had the power to hire and fire staff. Soon she'd become my trusted confidant and the mother of my son.

The office attendant entered with the coffee and laid it on the side table.

"The usual mix, Mr. Dan?" She asked.

"Yes," I answered without looking at her. She poured me a cup and left.

I took a sip and buzzed Toni to come back into my office.

"Here is the file," she said, placing the file on my desk.

"You hold it," I stated. "Give me the total amount we transferred to them during the period."

She scanned the file and stopped at the last entry.

"Fifty million US dollars," she said.

"Okay, you can leave."

She sat. "I need to talk to you about the accounts."

"What about them?"

"Several people have requested the return of their funds. Others have stopped incoming wires to their account."

"Why?"

"They heard we are closing down."

"What did you tell them?"

"I told them no."

"What are you worried about?"

"Nothing."

"Get to work then."

She got up to leave, pausing again at the door to survey me before returning to her station.

Tom came through the door smiling.

"Tell me the good news," I said.

He walked to the side bar, poured a cup of coffee, and sat. "I spoke to the minister of finance. He understands our position. We need to deliver the eight hundred million within ten days."

"That should give us enough time."

"Yes."

"What are they accusing us of?"

"The whole works. Money laundering, mail fraud, wire fraud, tax evasion, and running a Ponzi scheme. All serious charges."

"Who is behind this?"

"The British and the European Union, supported by the United States."

"Should we try to stop them?"

"First, we need to secure you." Tom looked around the office. "Anything we need to take from here?"

I dipped into my office drawer and pulled out two files. "Only these," I said, handing over the files to Tom.

"Let's go," he said.

Before we left, I walked to the other end of my office to a corner where I could see the staff in action without them seeing me. They were working. There were over twenty of them. Most of them were Toni's friends looking for easy money and the prestige of working in a bank. Raw and untrained—ideal mugs. Still working hard, still believing they were doing important transactions. I knew soon they would go home. They would learn this was an elaborate sham—but not from me.

I flicked a tear off my cheek with my finger as I turned away from the glass. I followed Tom through the back door. The driver was standing by the car with the engine running. Toni sped out of the office towards me. Her long strides got her to the car, trapping me before I could enter.

"What is wrong with you today, Dan?" Her dark eyes bore into me. "You did not even ask how your son is doing today."
I grimaced. "Call you later. I must go now." Tom and I entered the car and left.

We cruised out of the parking lot and onto the road home.
The phone in the car rang. "You knew I would check up on you," my sister Rita said. "How are you feeling today? How is your hip? Did you take your medication?"

"I did," I lied. In my haste to meet the prime minister this morning, I'd forgotten to take my medication. Rita's nurse training did not allow her to ignore my health.

"Make sure you get some rest," she said. "You cannot afford a relapse. Remember, you are not in the United States. You are on an island with poor health facilities."

"With you calling all the time, I feel like I'm at home."
"So, you have no plans on ever coming back to Indiana?" she asked.
"No."

"You can still get back your surgeon's license to operate within a few states."

"I am not interested."

"I can speak to some influential people."

"Change the subject, Rita."

"How is your son? And his mother?"

"They are doing great," I said. "Sounds like you have grown to accept them."

"It takes time."

"They are part of my world now," I said. "My new world. Get used to that."

"I am trying," she said "We will talk again tomorrow. Bye, bye." She cut the line.

Rita meant well. She cared for me. Ten years after I'd lost my surgeon's license due to negligence and drug abuse, she still had not accepted my circumstances. My change of profession to an offshore banker and investor on a remote island remained unacceptable. Having a Harvard-trained surgeon as a brother sounded better.

She objected to my new life and relationships. She could not imagine me with a black girlfriend and a half-caste child. I'd invited her to come to the island for a vacation. She refused to come.

Even in her closeness, she maintained a distance. Whenever I sent her money, she returned it. Last month, I sent twenty thousand dollars and she refused to touch it. Yet she called every day to make sure I took my medication.

We arrived at the house and I took my medication. In no order, I popped one or two from each vial into my mouth and drank a few mouthfuls of water. I walked back to the verandah and sat in one of the rocking chairs. Tom sat in the other chair and worked the phones.

I must have dozed. I woke up smelling Chinese food. Tom was eating and grinning between mouthfuls of roasted chicken, twice-cooked pork, chunky vegetables, and fried noodles.

"I ordered enough for both of us," he said. "Your favorite."

"I am not hungry."

He continued eating. I stared at the lawn as it merged with the white sand beach and disappeared into the deep blue sea. I realized that I would miss this place. For once in my life, I lived in a tranquil, sedentary environment. I had everything I'd ever wanted here.

On one side of the bay, my neighbor was pulling his power launch from the water. On the other side, away from the beach and closer to the ridge, several new luxury villas were being developed for sale and lease to international investors.

I turned to face Tom. "Any progress?"

"My understanding is that there has been an international crackdown on offshore banking." He sipped coke and cleared his throat. "Under new arrangements with the Mutual Legal Assistance Treaty, countries like Sokas have signed off to discontinue all offshore banks and their related parties. The big countries see us as extracting too much money from their economies and setting up facilities for tax evasion."

"Bullshit."

"Not for them." Tom turned to stare at the ocean. "They think we are guilty."

"What do you suggest?"

"You should leave." He tore his eyes away from the sea and looked at me. "I will stick around. You can return as soon as I get matters under control."

"Book me a ticket."

"I would not suggest that." Tom's eyes met mine. "You will need a quiet, unreported exit." He shifted his gaze to our neighbor's motor launch.

"You think he would do it?"

"For a few dollars more?" Tom laughed.

"I am game." I felt relaxed. This was a temporary setback. Soon, I would be back on my favorite island, relaxing and enjoying my semi-retirement.

"I will talk to him," Tom said.

Tom was driving out of the yard when Toni walked in with Josh.

"Daddy, Daddy!" He rushed towards me.

I hugged him from where I sat. "Every time I see you, you look taller and heavier," I said.

"Mommy tells me I am a growing kid," he said with a British accent. The expensive international private school was paying off.

"Go inside," I said. "Play a game on my computer. I need to talk to your mom."

"Thanks, Dad. That will be awesome," he said, running away.

I turned to Toni. "What are you doing here? And why did you bring him?"

"I did not like your attitude this morning," she said. "You were strange."

"So, you come here?"

"I didn't mean to upset you, Dan," she claimed.

"What do you expect to gain by coming here?"

"What is happening with you?" she asked.

"There is nothing going on," I said. "Take the boy and bring him back to your house. You cannot stay here."

"OK," she said. "Josh, let us go."

"We only just got here Mommy."

"Your father is busy," she said. "Let us go."

Josh emerged. "Bye Daddy."

"Bye Josh," I said. "See you soon."

I looked toward the ocean again. On my first trip to Sokas, I'd looked from the private jet, wondering if I was seeing the entire island. I'd asked the pilot to fly over a second time.

On the second round, I appreciated the exquisiteness of the place. A small Garden of Eden tucked away from the madding crowd.

The motor launch pulled up on the beach at two in the moonlit morning. I boarded with only the clothes I was wearing, a computer bag containing my laptop and files, and a suitcase full of US dollars.

I waved Tom goodbye and we pulled out. It was a simple plan. The launch would get me to the coast of Venezuela in four hours. From there, I'd hire a private jet to take me to my haven in Omanbutu. As the coast of Sokas disappeared in the distance, I hobbled downstairs and sat on the bed in the stateroom, trying to relax.

I'd been in Omanbutu for one week and I still hadn't heard a word from Tom. Rita could not call me, and I dared not let her know where I was. By now, I missed the bank and its trappings. I missed Toni and Josh.

We got newspapers from London and the United States. I did not make the headlines in the large publications. But, in the financial news section, there was mention of - *a Ponzi scheme worth five hundred million US dollars* operated by Dan Singular and his Singular Bank on the island of Sokas.

The noise from the helicopter gunship woke me at four that morning. The gunships landed one hundred meters from the compound. Soldiers disembarked and sprinted towards us.

They were everywhere. They broke into the building from four angles and were onto me before I could put on my clothes.

I offered no resistance. They hogtied me, naked and shivering, and tossed me into a helicopter. Within minutes, we were airborne.

THE END

The Magistrate

The magistrate, Delroy Ramsey, is sitting on his bench listening to the police prosecutor, Sergeant Elaine Shipman, present her case. Ramsey is trying hard to focus on her delivery as the effects of the Black & White whisky from the night before attacks his concentration. He looks around the packed courtroom, twisting his head and blinking his eyes behind his transition lenses to keep focus. He straightens himself in his high-backed chair to ease his discomfort.

"Your Worship, in concluding, the State is asking for the maximum sentence for the defendant. We know him as a regular, persistent offender and no stranger to the authorities. We have made our case. This man must remain in custody," the prosecutor states and sits.

"Counsel?" Ramsey beckons to the defense attorney.
Roger Baynes, the defense attorney, continues to shuffle through his papers on his desk, ignoring the magistrate.

"Counsel!" Ramsey shouts.

Baynes places his papers in order and rises to his feet. He snaps the bright red suspenders visible under his open jacket and takes a few steps toward the bench. He stops halfway.

"Your Worship, if I may, we have nothing to say," he states. "The prosecution has failed to present their case against my client. They presented not a single witness in this case. They came to you with a series of conjecture, suppositions, and innuendo. The defense has weaved together a pattern of lies, brought it to you, and called it a case. This cannot be a case—they have no case." He sits.

"I am ready to rule," the magistrate states. "Do any of you have additional presentations?"

"I have nothing further Your Worship," the prosecutor states, half-rising from her seat.

"Your Worship." Baynes rises from his seat and begins his short walk towards the bench. "They have not presented to this court the two hundred grams of cocaine said to be in my client's possession. Where is the evidence? Your Worship, this is a simple formula: no witnesses, no evidence, no case."

The defense attorney turns before reaching the bench and returns to his seat.

"Case dismissed. I am standing down all other matters for today until tomorrow." Ramsey lifts his hammer and slams it on the bench.

"All rise." The court clerk shouts. The people in the public gallery stand as the magistrate leaves the court.

Ramsey leaves the courthouse through the back. He crosses the road and enters the bar. He walks up to the counter and removes his gown, folding it and placing it on a nearby bar stool.

"Scotch," he demands. "My usual."

The barman places two cubes of ice in a glass and pours a measure of Black & White whisky into it. "Your favorite, double dog." The barman smiles.

"The only scotch whisky there is," Ramsey says, taking a sip on the mix.

"To each his own poison," the barman states.

"You don't drink?"

"Nah, I only serve it."

"Keep it that way." Ramsey takes another sip. "Don't get like me."

"What are you?"

"I am a sinner and a hopeless drunk."

"That's what you say about yourself."

"I know myself."

"Does that make your advice good?"

"Another thing: don't appear before me."
The barman smiles and moves off to attend to another customer.

"What a brilliant performance." The magistrate turns to see Roger Baynes on a stool next to him. "Your turn to buy me a beer."

"Do I have a choice?" the magistrate asks. He opens his hand and Baynes places an envelope into it. "Barman, give Counsel a beer."

"What's on for later?" the attorney asks.

"I will try to stay home with the wife," the magistrate says, looking at the bottles on the shelf. "I will put in quality time."

"You guys patching things up?"

"Working on it my brother." The magistrate bows his head. "It is a work-in-progress. Women are unpredictable."

"Friend of mine says his wife is only happy when she is unhappy."

"He has a problem on his hands," the magistrate says. "What are your plans for later?"

"I have a few things to catch up on and then I will plan my next move." The attorney tosses the beer into the back of his throat and leaves the bar.

Ramsey consumes four more shots and leaves without paying the bartender.

The bartender watches him leave.

The magistrate drives to his home enters the house, placing his bag, robe, and the envelope on a side table. He sits to watch television. Within minutes, he falls asleep, snoring.

He wakes up to see his wife, Lena Ramsey, leaning over him, prodding him from sleep. Beyond her, he turns his head to see the lights in the house and the darkness in the garden.

"Are you joining me for dinner?" Lena asks.

"Yes." He shakes his head. "Let me freshen up."

He gets up and staggers to the bathroom.

Lena returns to the kitchen to finish her preparations for dinner. Within minutes, he joins her, dressed in a pair of jeans and a flowered shirt. They sit at the table.

"Will you say grace before the meal?" she asks.

"You know I don't believe in that," he says. "So why do you always ask me?"

"People change."

"Not me. I like an old half-penny," he boasts, knocking his chest. "Nothing can change me."

"A better cock than you crowed already and ended up in chicken soup," she says.

"Skip the lecture, let's eat," he says, grabbing the bowl of roasted chicken. He places two thighs on his plate. He devours the chicken, guzzles a cup of iced tea, and belches.

She bows her head in prayer. At the end of her prayer, she looks up to see him wiping his mouth with the table towel. He belches again.

"So how was your day?" she asks, taking salad from the mixing bowl.

"Do I have to answer that?"

"Not if you don't want to."

"Well you leave that alone."

"Eat the salad. It's good for you."

"Woman, they send you to provoke me?"

"I am only trying to help."

"I do not need your help."

They sit in silence while she munches her dinner. He drinks more iced tea and burps.

"I am going out," he says, breaking the silence.

"As usual," she says. "Have fun."

He rises from the table walks to the doorway, drags on his shoes, and leaves, slamming the door behind him. He drives out of the yard through a cloud of smoke from his burning tires.

Ramsey drives along the road from his house, passing through the junction without stopping, and pulls up at the front of his local watering hole. He climbs out of the car and enters the bar. The barman sees him coming and pours out his usual.

"Double it," Ramsey states.

The barman doubles the drink, scrutinizing the magistrate.

Ramsey lifts his head and empties the drink into the back of his throat.

"Another," he croaks out.

"No," the barman states.

"How you mean, no?" Ramsey cocks back his head.

"I am not giving another drink," the barman maintains.

"You're not giving me a drink? I have my money."

"I am not selling to you. Go home."

"I came from home."

"Then go somewhere else."

"Okay then." Ramsey tosses money on the counter and leaves the bar.

The barman gathers the money and pushes it into the drawer without counting it. "A magistrate," he mutters to himself.

Ramsey pulls up outside the nightclub, exits his car, and enters the club without paying. The doorman and the security watch him pass. On the inside, he goes to the bar and orders Black & White whisky on the rocks.

He turns from the barman to survey the dance floor. He sips on the scotch, peering into every corner. The floor is getting crowded. To one side, he sees a girl dancing by herself. He signals to her. She joins him by the bar.

"Can I offer you a drink?" he asks.

"Sure."

"What do you drink?"

"The barman knows."

He signals to the barman. The barman comes over and pours a glass of Moët.

"Thank you," she says.

 "Cheers."

They knock glasses.

"Want to dance?" he asks.

She nods.

They groove to the rhythm of the songs on the dance floor and return to the bar. They spend the next hour drinking and chatting with intermittent dancing on the floor.

"Let us go somewhere else," he suggests.

"Sure," she agrees.

They leave the party and walk to his car. They enter the car and drive away.

"Where are we going?" she asks as they drive away from the main party places.

"Somewhere safe," he says. "Sit back and enjoy the ride."

"I thought you were taking me to another party."

"I never said so."

"Take be back to the club."

"That is not possible."

"Take me back to the club." The tone of her voice forces him to look at her. It is too late; the spray from the tear gas tube in her hand blinds him. He turns back to focus on the road only to see a shadow flash across the car. From the sickening thud, he knows he has hit something. He'd hit the accelerator instead of the brakes. The car speeds into the cane field and stops as it sinks into the soft mud.

The tapping on the window on the driver's side wakes him. He sees the shadow of the policeman through the glass against the sunlight streaming through the cane field.

"Mr. Ramsey, you have to come with us," the policeman says.

Together, they open the door and Ramsey tries to get out. He winces in pain as he sits in the car. Two paramedics carry a stretcher to the car and roll him onto it. They take him away from the scene. In the hospital, he wakes up to see Lena sitting by his bedside.

"Where am I? What happened?" he asks.

"You are in the hospital," she says. "You ran off the road."

He tries to sit up but flops back onto the bed. He sees his right leg in a white cast and his wrist wrapped in bandages.

"My leg?"

"It's broken in two places."

He looks around and sees a policeman stationed at the entrance to his ward. "What is he doing there?"

"They say you are a flight risk."

"Flight risk?" He looks at his leg and grins.

"You killed a man."

"I did what?"

"You hit a man and killed him when you ran off the road."

"Am I being charged?"

"Yes."

"Oh my God."

"Yes, I will pray for you." She smiles.

A nurse enters the ward and signals for Lena to leave. Lena steps away from the bed while the nurse pulls the screen around Ramsey. She walks past the policeman and leaves the ward. The nurse goes through her routine, checking Ramsey's temperature, blood pressure, bandages, and the speed of his drips.

"Nurse, did a strange girl come to visit me?"

The nurse looks at him and smiles. "Several strange girls came to visit you while you were out. What does she look like?"

"Petite. Fine bones. Pretty."

"About fifteen?"

"I don't know her age."

"She is fourteen," the nurse confirms. "I told her not to come back."

Ramsey looks at the nurse. She reopens his screen and leaves to visit the next patient.

In the magistrate's court, Magistrate Vaughn Wilson is presiding, Elaine Shipman is on her feet for the prosecution, Delroy Ramsey is sitting in the defendant's chair holding onto his crutches for balance, and defense attorney Roger Baynes is sitting next to him, studying his papers.

"Your Worship, the defendant in this case, your colleague, an attorney at law and an officer of this court, faces very serious charges. The State intends to make an example of him. We intend to uphold the law and to show that the law is for everybody. The law applies to everyone. Those who intend to use their position to abuse the law will feel the full weight of our justice system.

"The evidence will show that on the night in question Mr. Ramsey drove his car in a reckless and unlawful manner, endangering the lives of bystanders, killing a pedestrian, and almost killing himself. He did this while under the influence of alcohol, with an expired driving license, and with unpaid insurance. That said night, he attempted to rape a minor, who escaped.

"We will seek the maximum sentence in this case without leniency." She walks back to her desk and sits.

Magistrate Wilson looks at Roger Baynes. Baynes continues to read.

"Defense counsel?" Magistrate Wilson croons.

Baynes rises to his feet and looks around at the public gallery, the prosecutor, and then to Magistrate Wilson.

"Your Worship, this is a peculiar case. It could happen to any of us," he begins.

"Counsel." Magistrate Wilson is furious. "Watch your language."

"Your Worship, it could have been me."

"That's better," Magistrate Wilson states. "Please proceed."

"This is an officer of the court; a law-abiding citizen of this country. He finds himself a victim of the system. Let me remind the court that my client is innocent until proven guilty. He was tried and convicted in the court of public opinion. Examine the crowd here today. The evidence will show that my client has paid all his fees, charges, and taxes up to date. It will also show that when he picked up the young lady in the nightclub, he had no reasonable way of knowing she was under the legal age to be in the club. Regarding the alcohol limit, the police did not test my client for alcohol at the time of the accident.

"Their entire case is a sham. I intend to prove that." Baynes sits.

"You are both aware of my role in this situation," Magistrate Wilson states. "I have no authority to decide this case. I must form an opinion, based on the evidence, of whether sufficient evidence was presented to enable the matter to go to the high court. In sending the matter to the high court, I am allowing the defendant a trial by a judge and a jury of his peers.

"It is my judgement that this matter goes to the high court for a full trial. In the meantime, the defendant will be in custody while awaiting trial."

Baynes rises to his feet. "Your Worship, I request bail for my client."

The prosecutor jumps to her feet. "The prosecution objects."

Magistrate Wilson looks at Baynes. "Explain why your client needs bail."

"My client is a first-time offender. He is an exemplary citizen of this country. He has served this nation in several capacities with great distinction. My client is not a flight risk."

Magistrate Wilson looks at the prosecutor.

"He has the opportunity to flee. He will use his extensive connections around the world to find a safe haven."

Magistrate Wilson slams his hammer. "I set bail at one million dollars with two sureties."

"All rise," the guard shouts.

Magistrate Wilson leaves the courthouse.

Two policemen lead Ramsey out of the court.

Ramsey is on the remand block surrounded by four other prisoners. He looks around at the men and they stare back at him. Ramsey secures a corner of the cell and rolls himself into a ball.

THE END

Brother B

The incessant ring of the telephone woke me. I must have dozed off with the M52 rifle still across my lap. I was keeping watch through the night at the militia base. I ran to the phone.

The voice on the line was shouting, panicking, inaudible. "Calm down, man," I croaked. "Speak slowly so I can understand what you are saying."

"A yacht," the man managed. "It have ah yacht."

"Where is it?"

"In the harbor."

"Which harbor?"

"Halifax."

"Thanks." I replaced the telephone.

"Comrades, let's move." I barked out the order. I looked around to see Doggie dragging on his sneakers and jumping to attention. At the other end of the room, Brother B was crawling out of his sleeping bag and stretching.

"Major, I need to pee before we move."

"Move it," I shouted at him.

They called me Major not because of rank. In the militia, we had no rank. Major was a shortening of Major Haddad, the head of the Free Lebanon Army fighting in the Gaza Strip. Major Haddad was a military strongman who'd been dismissed from the Lebanese

Army for his connection to the Israeli Army. Back then, the exploits of Walid Jumblatt (leader of the Lebanese Druze Militia), Major Haddad, and Menachem Begin (the Israeli prime minister) had dominated the air waves.

Personally, I did not accept that any of my actions had been like Major Haddad's, but the name stuck with me. The name arose from my command of the camp and my tendency to take control of our routine operations. The men respected me and responded to my command. I always showed them respect and sincerity.

My real name was Bertie Jones and, like the other comrades, I dedicated my nights to serving in the People's Militia. I served four nights per week and even on my nights off I was available and on call. I attended college by day and picked up my rifle by night.

The militia was a peoples' force supplementing the People's Revolutionary Army (PRA). Our task was securing the village and the surrounding areas and taking care of minor breaches of security. In addition, we were there to serve as a backup force to the PRA during an invasion of the island by foreign forces. Where an incident developed beyond our ability, we'd need to call in the army and allow them to solve the problem.

Brother B scurried outside and descended the stairs toward the pit latrine at the back of the militia camp. He urinated outside the small hut.

He came back up the stairs.

"You ready?" I looked at him.

"As soon as ah get me gun."

He walked to the gun rack, selected an Enfield .303 rifle, checked the small magazine, stuffed a few bullets into his pocket, and walked back toward us.

The three of us moved out of the door and climbed into the Suzuki J10 parked at the foot of the stairs on the main road outside the militia building.

It was a two-story concrete building off-set from the center of the junction in Concord, where four roads met. We called it the 'four road.' On reflection, it was not four roads but a crossing of two roads; the western main road from Queen's Park to the town of Sauteurs was crossed by the Concord mountain road running from the Concord waterfalls to the black sand beach at Black Bay.

I'd grown up in the Concord valley among a mixture of agricultural production and tourist attractions. In the mountains, banana, nutmegs, cloves, and a variety of spices thrived under the cover of the rainforest's canopy, and there were three of the most amazing waterfalls on the island. On the other end, by the sea, by one of the few black sand beaches on the island, were the dry lands, which were ideal for sugar cane and sweet potatoes.

We were young, free-spirited, and eager to help. The revolution gave us the opportunity to serve our country and enhance its security. We took up the challenge and made ourselves available. It was, for us, a spirit of friendship and comradeship.

The PRA took control of the house after the revolution and turned it into a militia camp. Upstairs served as sleeping quarters while we cooked and entertained ourselves on the ground floor.

During the day and into the nights, we played dominoes and cards and the odd game of chess.

I cranked up the motor, put it into gear, and drove out.

"Wait. Wait," Brother B shouted.

"What the ass?" Doggie barked at him.

"My jacket." Brother B was apologetic. Doggie glared at him. "Ah need me jacket. Ah feeling cold already."

I stopped the Suzuki and Brother B jumped out and disappeared into the darkness.

I wondered if Brother B was not up to a prank. I remembered when, as a child, he'd come home from London and performed practical jokes on us. He'd had this camera that he took our pictures with. He'd then wave his hands in the air magically and within seconds show us our photos. Several years later, we realized that he'd been using a Polaroid instant camera.

He ran back to us, struggling to get his hands into the thick, heavy, British-made woolen jacket.

"What is it wid you and this bush jacket?" Doggie snarled at him.

Brother B snuggled himself into the jacket and smiled. "It keeps me warm and tender through the night," he sang, holding his belly and wriggling up against his hands. "You don't know about these things. You never sleep wid ah woman yet."

Doggie pursed his thick lips.

"You know, Brother B is not a simple man Doggie," I chimed in as I pulled away from the militia building again. "He is an old Englishman. Loves his jacket. Loves to keep warm on a cold night."

"Tell him Major," Brother B echoed. "We have to teach the youth. Dem nah know nutting."

I took my eyes off the road and glanced over at Doggie. I could see his teeth glowing in the light of the quarter moon.

"Brother B is an Englishman," I said. "He spent most of his life in London. He was a member of the Royal Air Force."

"Brother B?" Doggie jeered.

"Have respect guy," I insisted. "He left Grenada at sixteen for Aruba. He worked on the island for a few years then returned home. Soon he got restless again and jumped the banana boat to England. He spent forty years in England."

"Dey say he was a vagrant over dey."

"Where you get that from?" I snapped.

"Da is wha dey say." Doggie was shameless. "Ah wasn't dey."

"So, shut up."

"Da is wha ah hear."

By then, we had climbed the hill into Cotton Baille and descended toward Woodford Corner. I stopped the van on the hill around the corner overlooking the harbor, and there it was: a small yacht, a single light at the top of its mast, bobbing in the shallow waters of Halifax Harbor.

The harbor itself was a natural formation set deep in the rocks of the west coast of the island. The opening was a narrow channel that opened wider as one sailed further into it. Located less than fifteen minutes cruising speed from the main yacht club in the island's capital, St. George, it was ideal for the odd yachtsman trying to evade the heavy holding charges in the city, searching for a different experience, or looking for the serenity and tranquility offered by the remote harbor.

Most of our operations were routine. We drove to the harbor, took a small fishing boat from storage on the beach, oared out to the yacht, requested their permission to board, boarded, and searched them. Most of them had become regulars and knew our routine. They had formed the habit of keeping a few supplies for us whenever we boarded.

I slipped the van into neutral and allowed it to crawl down the hill.

I stole a glance at Doggie. His long ears were flapping in the wind toward his deep-set eyes, and his long Alsatian mouth and matching teeth were outlined against the distant sky. *Whoever had first called him Doggie,* I thought, *had made no mistake.*

"Brother B, should I attempt to educate Doggie, or is it a waste of my time?"

"Continue, Major," Brother B stated, looking up into the hills. "You doing a good job, comrade."

At eighteen, Doggie was two years older than me, but our lives had taken different paths. Doggie had disappeared from school when we were in standard four, two years before we were due to sit the entrance exams for secondary school. We never got the full story, but I recall the headmaster ordering Doggie to report to his office for a beating.

Earlier that day, Charlie, our class teacher and the headmaster's son, had put Doggie and a few others out of the class for not doing their homework. The last time I'd seen Doggie that day, he'd been walking along the track behind the school, heading toward his mother's house.

The next day, Charlie, who rode a motorbike to class, showed up with several plasters on his head.

Charlie had found no sympathy among us. His father brought him to teach us, at age sixteen, as soon as he left school with his school leaving certificate. Other people in the village who had attained secondary and tertiary education and had applied for the job had failed, and Charlie had showed up to teach.

"Brother B was one of the first Grenadians to purchase a house in London. He had problems with his marriage and, during that time, the bank repossessed the property and sold it for less than it was worth. He challenged the bank in court. During that time, he slept rough. The case took twenty-five years to conclude. He won. He collected the compensation and came to Grenada."

"Ah din know dat," Doggie stated.

"You didn't ask," I pointed out.

I slipped the vehicle back into gear as it ran out of momentum on the flat leading to the access road to the harbor. Doggie looked at Brother B with fresh admiration.

"Sorry Brother B," he consoled. "I didn't know. You had such a hard life. No wonder you a fighter wid us in the struggle today."

"I forgive your ignorance, ole chap," Brother B stated.

I killed the light and turned onto the road leading to the beach at the harbor. I allowed the vehicle to roll onto the incline to the beach and parked in the bushes at the edge of the bay. We climbed out, clutching our rifles, and moved across the beach to select a fishing boat. We took a small oaring boat, slid it along the sand, and launched it into the water, jumping in as it left the shore.

Doggie took the oars, rowing the boat across the water toward the anchored yacht. We must have been halfway to the yacht when they turned on a blinding spotlight. A gunshot rang out, shattering the silence of the night. Doggie panicked, let go of the oars, and jumped overboard. Brother B followed, clutching his Enfield .303 rifle.

I hesitated. Another gunshot echoed against the rocks of the valley behind me and something hit the water. I needed no further persuasion. I followed them, tossing my body into the water and holding onto my M52 rifle. The water shocked me, and I felt my legs cramping. I released the M52 and kicked hard at the water. I could not feel my right leg.

With my hands and my left leg, I swam underwater for several feet before surfacing for air and diving underwater again. Within minutes, I was crawling up the shore and into the bushes, out of range of the light from the yacht.

"Major." I heard Doggie's shaky whisper inches away from my position.

"Yes," I croaked out. "Where is Brother B?"

"No sight ah him."

"We will give him a few minutes," I said. We waited for several minutes. "Let's return to base. He will find his way back."

We crawled through the bushes back to the vehicle. The yacht killed the light. I started the Suzuki and raced back to camp.

Back at the camp, we dried ourselves off and changed into dry clothes.

I sat on the stairs, staring into the cocoa trees across the way. I could not get my mind off Brother B. He had this special relationship with my father. My father always read through his schemes and cast them off as jokes. I remembered one of those days when he'd come to the back door of our house on the kitchen side to sell crayfish to my father. They were huge, lovely crayfish, the best in the river. My father frowned at him.

"How do you hold these?"

He laughed. "Knowledge, technique, and fearlessness."

"Nobody else seems to catch these."

Brother B raised up his hands. "These are delicate, secure, and reliable."

"You so full of yourself." My father smiled.

"These hands of mine trod where others fear to tread." Brother B curled his hands through the air. "They move into the dark recesses under the stones seeking the ling and *Guage*. These hands are no *Cacado* and *redtail* hands. When ah hold *lamae* and *latchae*, ah does throw dem back in the river."

"Tell me something Brother B," my father queried. "How come you always sell them half-cooked?"

Brother B laughed. "They last longer when they scalded."

My father shook his head. "You are a scamp." He handed Brother B five dollars and took the plastic bag of crayfish. Brother B bowed and scurried away.

My father looked at me. "You know what he does?"

"No."

"His theory is that the real nutrients and vitality are in the crayfish sauce and not the flesh. He scalds them and drinks the water then sells the flesh."

"Jesus."

"Precisely."

Doggie came to join me outside. He could not sleep either. An hour had passed since we'd returned to camp, and there was still no sight of Brother B. I reported to the regional commander. His advice was to wait, tell no one, and await the break of day, when visibility would improve. He said that, knowing Brother B, he would be back in the camp by then, kicking up a rumpus about being deserted by his troops.

The commander and two other men arrived at daybreak as promised. We sped to the harbor and pulled up on the beach, guns at the ready and prepared to shoot. The yacht had gone along with the small fishing boat. One of the commander's men stripped to his trunks and picked up a snorkel and a pair of goggles.

"First, try without tanks," the commander stated.

I climbed into a bigger fishing boat with the commander and the man in trunks and we oared out toward the spot where Brother B had disappeared. The man fitted on his snorkel and goggles and eased himself overboard. Within seconds, he resurfaced. He removed the glass and snorkel.

"I am seeing something. Give me some rope," he said.

The commander handed him a line of rope from the fishing boat. The man replaced his apparatus and dived. When he came back up, he signaled to us to oar toward the shore. The commander oared. Back on the shore, we pulled the boat out of the water and tugged on the rope, pulling in the weight at its end. Brother B emerged from the water. Fishes and crabs hung from his face and fingers.

He never stood a chance. He'd cramped as soon as he'd hit the water. His body was folded around the Enfield .303 rifle, and I knew its weight had dragged him to the bottom. As he'd sunk, the thick woolen coat had soaked up water, adding to the weight.

It was the first time I had seen a dead body. I ran back to the Suzuki and sobbed.

THE END

Father Freddy

When Shakira Talon kissed him on the lips in the living room of the presbytery that Wednesday evening while attending counselling, Father Freddy knew it was coming. He had known it was coming for four days now.

Last Sunday, he had delivered his troubled sermon at the church, and what a confusion he'd stirred up within the congregation and with Shakira Talon.

The priest recalled standing at the pulpit that morning and surveying the congregation. He looked at the weary, expectant faces focused on him, looking to him for guidance and redemption. He slid his prepared sermon into the cubbyhole in the pulpit and spoke from his heart.

"Parishioners, I will not address you using my prepared sermon this morning. This Sunday, I will share with you what is on my mind and in my heart. I want to converse with you today about what I carry around now. We will discuss my fears and insecurities."

The diminutive priest descended from the altar and walked toward the congregation. As he walked, the wireless microphone in his lapel continued to send his crisp voice through the church's speakers.

"Sisters and brothers, my feelings are not new, nor are they restricted. Priests have feelings. We know that, in Peter 5:8, the Bible tells us, 'Be alert and of sober mind. Your enemy the devil prowls around like a lion looking for someone to devour.' We find ourselves bombarded by negative forces attempting to devour our faith in the Lord. Pushing back our beliefs, tackling our support systems, undermining our duty, and messing with our minds."

He reached the back of the church and sat in an empty pew. "I have doubted my strength. Questioned my faith. Wondered whether I am a victim of weakness. A victim of doubt. Am I yielding to temptation? These questions have entered my mind. Negative thoughts inundated me. They have flooded my system and placed me in compromising situations. I am supposed to play a leading role in the church. I am supposed to provide guidance to the congregation. You should be able to come to your priest for direction. How is that possible when I doubt myself and my faith?

"I sought help in the words of the Lord. I looked to Corinthians 10:13, where the Bible tells us, 'No temptation has overtaken you except what is common to mankind. And God is faithful; he will not let you be tempted beyond what you can bear. But when you are tempted, he will also provide a way out so that you can endure it.'"

The priest stood up and began his walk back toward the pulpit.

"Please understand that, although I am a priest, I am first a man of flesh and blood. I only represent the Lord. I am not perfect. Only the Lord is omnipotent. I am human and capable of temptations common to mankind. But the Lord tells us he will not allow us to be tempted beyond what we can bear. He promises that he will provide a way out."

The priest climbed the altar. The eyes of the congregation bore into his back. He turned around and saw her. He knew her well. Shakira Talon: a regular, active churchgoer. She was staring straight through him as if he was not there. She had this glossy, dazed lack-of-an-expression on her face. The priest repeated himself: "But when you are tempted, he will also provide a way out, so you can endure."

He peeled his eyes away from her and cleared his throat, cracked open the little bottle of purified water, and sipped from it. Was the Lord sending him a signal? Could Shakira Talon be his way out? He tossed the thoughts from his mind and forced himself to focus on a small child at the center of the church.

"Sisters and brothers, in times like these we look to the Lord for strength, expecting him to carry us through. Isaiah 40:29 tells us, 'He gives strength to the weary and increases the power of the weak.' In times like these, we force ourselves to plow deep into our faith in search of a solution. Searching for that elusive answer to our doubts, using our strength and resolve to find one. We surrender ourselves to the Lord, allowing him to carry us through. Carry us to where we once were. We try to restore our fundamental principles."

"In Corinthians 4:9, we are told, 'Finally, brothers and sisters, whatever is true, whatever is noble, whatever is right, whatever is pure, whatever is lovely, whatever is admirable–if anything is excellent or praiseworthy–think about such things.' In the next few days, I will consider such things. I will surrender myself to the mercies of the Lord and I know his wishes will prevail.

"Sisters and brothers, I thank you and I ask that you mention me in your prayers."

Father Freddy signaled to the Deacon to continue the mass and left the hall.

He was in the kitchen of the presbytery making himself a cup of tea after the mass ended when he heard a light tapping on the entrance. He walked through the living room and opened the solid wooden door. Shakira Talon was standing there.

"Father, can I come in?" she asked, looking beyond the priest. "Do you have company? I need to talk to you."

"You can." He moved aside and allowed her to enter. "I was in the kitchen making myself some tea. Can I offer you a cup?"

"That would be great." She followed him into the kitchen.

He completed making the tea and offered her a cup. She followed him to the dining table, where they sat.

"Father, your preaching this morning moved me," she stated. "I feel blessed."

He blushed. "If you wish to call it that."

"Father, it was stirring."

"More the ramblings of a frustrated priest," he observed, gazing into his tea.

"I disagree," she said, trying to look him in the eye. "For years, I have attended this church and several others, and I have never been moved by a sermon. I am sure that if you had delivered your prepared text, it would not have had such a gripping effect on me."

"At least I am humbled by the knowledge that I have touched a soul."

"More than that, all the areas you touched on are affecting me and my marriage." Father Freddy recoiled.

"Father, it was as if you were looking straight through me, seeing my soul and addressing me. As if you knew all my problems. You stripped me naked before God."

"I can assure you that was not my intention," he said. He looked up, avoiding her eyes.

"My husband and I are having problems. The past few months have been difficult." She looked at her tea and took a sip. "I don't know where else to turn."

"Are you requesting a formal confession?"

She sipped on her tea. "No. I need to talk to someone." She lifted her eyes again. "As a friend."

"I am not capable of this." He held her eyes. He could see the tears trickling down her cheeks. "I can take formal confessions where anything you say will be between you and me and God. Or I can treat it as a counselling session. I think I can counsel parishioners."

"Treat it as you wish. I need your listening ear."

"Okay, Wednesday at five p.m."

"I'll see you then." She forced a smile. She drank the remainder of her tea and left.

In the afternoon, Father Freddy picked up his mother from the home for the aged and drove her to the beach. He sat on a stone while she pattered around in the shallow waters. He took her out of the home as regularly as his work at the church allowed.

They left the beach to drive back to the home. His mother looked at him. "You are rather quiet today son," she said. "That is not like you."

"Yes, I have matters weighing me down."

"What will you do?"

"I don't know."

"Why not discuss it with one of your fellow priests?"

"Never." The priest stole a look at his mother. "They would not understand, Mom."

"Then try a woman," she suggested.

"A woman? What woman?"

"Try a nun," she said. "There was one who encouraged you during your pupilage."

"Sister Alma."

"Yes. Talk to her."

He laughed for the first time. "Good idea Mother. I will visit her. Thank you."

"That's what I am here for."

"We must be gracious."

He dropped his mother off at the home.

On Monday afternoon, Father Freddy drove to the convent in Bocage to visit Sister Alma. When he arrived at the building, Sister

Alma was sitting in the veranda, chatting with Sister Shirley over afternoon tea.

They both greeted him and asked him to join them for their afternoon tea and chat. He accepted the nuns' invitation.

They spoke of the church and the changing environment in which they operated. They discussed the evolving congregation and the need for strategies in carrying out the will of God.

"You don't seem to be yourself father," Sister Alma stated out of the blue.

"I am not," Father Freddy replied, staring away from the nuns and into the long, deep, green valley. "I think I am doubting my faith." He explained to them his experience in the church last Sunday morning and the strange thoughts he had been having.

The nuns exchanged glances as he spoke.

"Is there a woman involved?" Sister Alma asked.

"No. Not at all." Father Freddy paused. "Well, not yet." "A woman visited me after service," he said. "She said she wanted counselling. But there is something about her. Can't explain what it is."

"She is the devil," Sister Shirley blurted out. "The devil is dangling the world before you. The Bible tells us in Luke 22:40, 'On reaching the place, he said to them, pray that you will not fall to temptation.' Be careful, father."

"Sisters, I am willing to follow your advice." He refocused on the nuns.

"Go to the bishop," Sister Shirley stated. "He will know what to do."

"I agree," Sister Alma said.

"I will heed your advice sisters," the priest stated. "I will visit the fountain of the church."

He spent the rest of the afternoon with the sisters chatting. They reminisced. They discussed the changing nature of the church. As the darkness descended on the village and a hint of condensation covered the valley, limiting visibility, Father Freddy stood up to leave.

Before he left, Sister Alma went into the convent and returned with a bronze scarf with a peculiar emblem embroidered into one end. She placed it around his neck, allowing it to cover the front of his shirt.

"This will protect you," she said.

He accepted the symbol of protection and left.

The next afternoon, he travelled to the Bishop's residence. On his way, he reflected on their suggestions. They were correct; it was a pity he had not seen it that way at once. The bishop was the spiritual leader of the church. His role was to offer temporal and spiritual leadership to priests and believers. Not only must he lead and oversee spiritual ideas, he must give divine inspiration. The priest recalled the Epistle of Ignatius in Ephesians 6:1: "Plainly therefore we ought to regard the bishop as the Lord himself."

A nursing assistant led him into the hallway of the bishop's official residence. Freddy followed him to the room at the end, which had been changed into a mini-hospital to accommodate the bishop. His skin tingled as he approached the open doorway. He stepped into the room.

The priest shivered, although he saw the nurse was sweating. He knew the bishop was ailing but did not know the extent of his illness. As he approached the bishop's bed, the nursing assistant powered up the head, enabling the bishop to sit upright.

He greeted the priest with a warm smile. The priest relaxed.

The bishop spoke about his terminal illness and the procedures the doctors had done. Father Freddy questioned him on his faith—how had he endured the daily pain and sporadic medical procedures? The bishop explained to the priest that, during his treatment, he had maintained his faith in the Most High. God was the master, even of bishops.

Father Freddy explained his crisis to the bishop. As he spoke, he attempted to read the emotions on the bishop's expressionless face. The bishop remained deadpan throughout. Robin paused to hear the bishop's views.

"You need to take some time away," the bishop said. "You need to find yourself."

"But bishop, where would I go?" Father Freddy protested. "The church is my life."

The bishop made himself comfortable in the bed and lowered his voice. "John 9:4: 'I must work the works of him who sent me while it is day; night is coming when no one can work.'"

The priest felt the sadness creeping through the bishop's voice. The bishop's message was plain. He felt guilty. He informed the bishop that he was leaving.

"As you go father, remember Proverbs 16:9: 'the heart of a man plans his way, but the Lord establishes his steps.'"

Father Freddy was relieved. He had the advice of people he respected. Now the Lord must do his job. He would pray and offer his weakness to the master. He was fortunate to have the nuns by his side. They had pointed him in the right direction. The bishop's wisdom clarified his confusion and relaxed him. The Lord would show him a way to follow.

On Wednesday evening, the priest took a long, warm shower, put on a pair of slacks and a multi-colored shirt, and slid his feet into a pair of leather slippers. He read a book and sipped cold water while he waited for Shakira Talon to arrive.

The light tap on the door was two hours late. He opened the door. Shakira slid past him, bouncing his hand with her bottom.

"Madame, you are late." The priest attempted to sound stern.

"I had to make sure you were ready," she said, turning around and dropping her house coat.

The priest had no time to react. She stepped toward him, held him around his waist, and kissed him.

He allowed his book to fall to the ground.

THE END

The British Slacker

I relax into my leather seat in the upper deck—premium economy—of the Virgin Atlantic 747-400 and close my eyes. The plane soars at a forty-five-degree angle into the sky over Gatwick Airport, London. I loosen my belt and pull my Ralph Lauren polo shirt out of my pair of Levi 501 jeans.

My eyes stay shut as the huge plane continues to climb to its cruising altitude. The smooth hum of the engines and the comforting whiz of the air conditioning cause me to dose off for a few minutes.

I wake up to find I am clutching the in-flight magazine, sitting in the window seat of the cabin. The plane reaches its cruising altitude, gliding across the sky.

I fiddle with the remote control for the television screen on the headrest in front of me.

"Can I offer you a drink of your choice, sir?" The air host is standing in the aisle, clutching a stack of menus in his hand. "I am Jaden and I will be your host for this flight to Grenada with a short stop-off in Tobago."

"I will have orange juice."

"You can look at the menu now to decide on lunch, Mr. Nelson," Jaden says, handing me a menu from his stack.

"Now that's what I call service."

"We distinguish ourselves with our personal touch, Mr. Nelson," Jaden states.

"I can see that."

"I will be back with your orange juice and to take your lunch order." He turns to the woman sitting next to me. "I would like to offer you a drink, Mrs. Corbin," he says. "This is the lunch menu. Please read and make your selection. I will take that order when I return with the drink."

She lifts her head from the pages of the duty-free shopping catalog. "I will have a glass of wine."

"Red or white?"

"Red."

"With the red you have a choice of a Merlot or a Cabernet Sauvignon."

"I will have the Cabernet Sauvignon."

"With the Cabernet Sauvignon you can have a Chilean or a French."

"I am used to the French at home. I will experiment with the Chilean."

"Coming straight up." Jaden returns to his station at the front of the plane.

I scrutinize her. She is wearing an ivory-colored, cotton-linen blend, custom-made designer jacket over a cotton vest with matching shorts. The jacket is ruffled around the waist and has silver metallic stripes at the edges. It is shoulder-padded, with elbow length sleeves and a two-button front.

She looks fifty-something, well kept, stuck-up, and expensive to support. Her gold Rolex watch glints in the cabin light every time she flicks her left hand. Around her neck and on her right hand, she

97

is wearing a glassy substance I don't recognize. She continues to flick the pages of the duty-free shopping catalog.

"Ladies and gentlemen, this is your captain speaking. My name is Nathan Farrell and I am in command of the aircraft for your long flight to Grenada, with a short stop in Tobago. Alongside me is First Officer Bob Rowe. We have reached our cruising altitude of thirty thousand feet, which we will maintain until we approach the Caribbean. The weather there is a warm twenty-eight degrees, falling to around twenty-four degrees at night.

"Not much to see on the outside. Lots of entertainment on the inside. I urge you to make use of it. Please sit back, relax, and enjoy the flight. In the event you need any help, press the flight attendant button above your head and someone will be there to help you. Goodbye for now folks. I will check in with you later in the flight."

I put my headphones on and choose *The Matrix Reloaded* to watch. Jaden returns with our drinks. I order steak with sauté potatoes and vegetables. The lady orders the same.

I return to my movie. She places her magazine in the seat pocket and uses her remote control to flick through the movie menu, sipping on her red wine.

It helps if you had seen *The Matrix* before watching *The Matrix Reloaded*, but it's not essential. Laurence Fishburne teams up with Keanu Reeves again to deliver another installment of sci-fi mastery.

Six months after the events depicted in *The Matrix*, Neo continues to be a good omen for the free humans. More humans are being freed from the Matrix and brought to Zion, the one and only stronghold of the resistance.

Neo, now possessing powers such as super speed, the ability to fly, and the ability to see the code embedded in the Matrix, finds out his role as the One. He experiences nightmares of Trinity being killed.

News hit the human resistance that 250,000 machine sentinels are digging to Zion and will reach them in seventy-two hours. As Zion prepares for the ultimate war, Neo, Morpheus, and Trinity try to find the Key-maker to help them reach the Source. Agent Smith escaped deletion and becomes more powerful than before. He chooses Neo as his next target.

My neighbor selects *Scooby-Doo* and giggles.

I doze off again just at the point where Agent Smith is trying to absorb Neo (without success).

"Mr. Nelson, please lay out your table. Lunch is ready," Jaden says.

I open my eyes and pull the table out of its storage. By then, Neo is flying to save Trinity, who is falling from a building. My neighbor is giggling away at the antics of *Scooby-Doo* and his friends.

Jaden returns to set the table. He lays out the linen table-cloth; china; stainless steel cutlery; and servings of fresh bread, butter, garden salad, salad dressing, and Perrier water. I wipe my hands with the warm damp towel, stretch my legs out, apply the creamy blue cheese dressing to my salad, and munch.

My neighbor ignores the salad and orders more wine.

Our meals arrive, and we eat in silence. The steak comes with a Greek salad of cucumbers, feta, oregano, and olive oil and vinegar dressing. The sauté potatoes lie in a bed of aubergine parmigiana with a crumbling cheese and herb topping.

My movie is over, so I switch to the radio to listen to vintage British radio comedy. The Two Ronnies lay into one of their favorites, "Four Candles." Ronnie Corbett runs an old ironmonger's store, and greets a customer (Ronnie Barker) who asks for what sounds like "four candles." Corbett provides four candles. Barker shows he misinterpreted what he said, stating that he asked for "fork handles—'andles for forks," meaning garden forks. Barker continues to ask for other items from a list and grows more and more frustrated as Corbett continues to misinterpret what he says.

My neighbor is into her second movie, *Scooby-Doo and the Monster*, and is giggling.

Jaden clears our table and returns with dessert. There is cheesecake, Häagen-Dazs ice cream, and a choice of liqueur. I choose Drambuie. My neighbor chooses Cointreau.

I clean up with the moist sanitary cloth.

My thoughts drift away from the radio to recall my time in London on this trip. It had been strange for me to return to London stronger than the poverty-stricken student I used to be. I'd rented a car from the airport and drove around the city sightseeing, no longer the mini-cab driver hustling to earn a few quid to pay my tuition fees.

The bathroom in the suite at the Lansdowne hotel on Hyde Park Corner was bigger than my whole student boarding room. I feasted on the buffet breakfast at the hotel every morning. At dinner time, I ate with my associates at one fine dining restaurant or another—places I hadn't known even existed.

I spent two days in Brussels meeting with high-level delegates from the European Union (EU) to talk about aid for Grenada. The drawdown of aid packages was lagging several years behind, and the EU were eager to speed it up. Lagging arose due to problems on both sides. The EU disbursement procedure remained complicated and overly rigid. At the same time, the Caribbean countries found it tough to recruit and keep specialists with the time and knowledge to master the procedures.

The ambassador did not show up to meet me at the airport in Brussels, so I took a taxi. I should have become suspicious when the driver walked me to the carpark to get his car instead of picking me up curbside. As we approached the payment booth at the exit, he inched his car close to the rear of the vehicle in front. When the bar lifted to allow the vehicle ahead through, he revved up his car, racing through the lifted barrier before it lowered.

He proceeded along a series of off-roads on his approach to my hotel downtown. As he emerged from the bushes, I asked why he operated this way. He told me he did not have a license to run at the international airport and was taking a risk to earn a living. I paid and tipped him in honor of my struggling days driving a minicab in London.

Later when I met the ambassador, I told him my story. He told me I was lucky. He never trusted these men.

Our meetings in Brussels went as planned. The EU agreed to allow the government more time to meet their stringent application rules. They agreed to give training to the officers responsible for preparing the applications. They retracted their earlier threat to withdraw and reallocate the funds to Africa.

Back in London, I found time to visit Madame Tussauds and the Natural History Museum. I saw *The Phantom of the Opera*.

"It's called Swarovski," my neighbor says.

"What?" She'd caught me staring at her jewelry.

"My jewelry," she says. "You were looking at it. It's called Swarovski."

"It's beautiful."

"My husband loves to buy them for me," she states, lifting her hand to fiddle with her wedding ring.

"Where is your husband? Why are you travelling alone?"

"I will meet him in Tobago." She smiles, showing her expensive dental work.

"My name is Gene," I say. "Gene Nelson."

"I am Caiti," she says. "Caiti Corbin."

"A pleasure Caiti," I say.

"Same here," she says. She presses the button to summon the host.

I flick through the movie list and choose *Mystic River*. *Scooby-Doo* is over, so Caiti moves on to *Finding Nemo*. Jaden arrives, and she orders more wine.

"You don't watch these?" she asks, pointing at the screen.

"I have never tried."

"You should try," she states. "Adults can watch them."

"I will try one soon."

Jaden fills her glass with wine. I continue watching *Mystic River*. My thoughts drift away from the movie to my return home. I was not looking forward to it. I always welcome time away from my office and interaction with diverse people. At home, the monotony of the job can be depressing.

The jealousy is depressing. My colleagues say I rose too high, too fast through the ranks of the public service. At thirty, I am the permanent secretary and director general of the Ministry of Finance, and have ambassadorial status.

The Cabinet chose me to represent the government in many international forums and negotiations. Staff see me as a chosen one. A few respect my ascendancy, while others can't wait to see me fall.

"He is looking forward to seeing me," she says.

"Who?"

"My husband."

"What is he doing in Tobago?"

"He is a developer." She looks at me. "His name is John Corbin. You must have heard of him."

"No," I say.

I lied. I'd met the man. He'd come to Grenada to discuss a luxury condo project and golf course. I disliked him. He was a racist. He had no respect for black people. The project he'd proposed involved building three- and four-bedroom luxury condos on a 250-acre plot in a gated housing community. Investors could custom-build their condos at various points on the golf course. They could choose between a condo on the edge of the beach or further inland, away from the rusting effects of the sea.

Incentives including tax-breaks would market the investment, along with straightforward purchasing, value for money pricing, and the lure of owning a vacation spot in the Caribbean.

We'd rejected the proposal on several grounds including: the need to cut trees, the destruction of agricultural crops and lands, the run-off of pesticides and other chemicals used on the golf course, leachate contamination of ground water sources, high amounts of water consumption, poor sewer treatment, and the gated housing community concept. Foreigners segregating themselves in housing communities hidden from the local population is an arrangement alien to the people of Grenada.

"He is working on building luxury condos and a golf course in Tobago."

"I see."

"He works hard, you know."

"I suspect."

"That's how I get to spend the money."

"How long will you be in Tobago?"

"Fourteen days."

"Have you been there before?"

"My first time."

"You will enjoy it."

"You think so?"

"Yeah."

A sudden sadness takes over her face. "Excuse me for a moment. I need to use the loo."

"Go ahead."

She stands and staggers toward the bathroom at the front of the plane. Jaden helps her enter the bathroom.

Back on *Mystic River*, Jimmy (Sean Penn) and his friends follow Dave (Tim Robbins) out of a bar. They corner him and question him about Kathie's (Jimmy's nineteen-year-old daughter) death. Jimmy admits to the killing, believing that the men will spare his life. Dave kills him and dumps him in the Mystic River.

Jaden helps Caiti stagger back to her seat. She sits.

"Bring me more wine," she says.

"Mrs. Corbin, I can't give you any more," Jaden says. "You've already had enough."

"Bring it or I will shout," she states.

Jaden goes to the front and returns with the wine. He fills her glass again.

"Leave the bottle," she demands.

"It is against regulations," he says.

"Leave it," she insists.

"I will allow it for once, but you must hide it."

"Fine."

She takes the three-quarters-full bottle and hides it among her belongings. Jaden walks to his station at the front.

I am absorbed in *Mystic River*.

Jaden hands out snacks. One package has a cheese and pickle finger sandwich, banana soufflé, cupcake, and fruit bowl. The fruit bowl has cubed chunks of assorted fruits, including mango, banana, green seedless grapes, melon, and apple. The other package has a granola bar, muffin, and a small orange juice.

We eat. I order a coffee. Caiti orders another Cointreau.

"Ladies and gentlemen, this is your captain once again. We are within ninety minutes of Tobago. Please use this opportunity to straighten up your belongings and to make that final visit to the washroom.

"The weather in Tobago remains warm and fair to cloudy, with a chance of isolated showers. If I don't speak to you again, it was a pleasure having you on board as always. We know you have many choices of airline, so we thank you for choosing Virgin Atlantic.

"For those of you leaving us in Tobago, enjoy your stay there. Passengers going to Grenada, we will be on the ground in Tobago for about forty minutes. Please stay on the aircraft. Use the opportunity to walk around and stretch your muscles.

"Enjoy your business trip or holiday. For those of you returning home, I trust you had a fine time overseas.

"So long, and it was a pleasure having you on board."

I take the hospitality pouch with its toothbrush and the tiny tube of toothpaste and sneak off to the washroom before the crowd hits it. Her eyes are on me. I return to my seat and relax.

"You are such a gentleman," she says. "You are not like him at all."

"Like who?"

"My husband," she cries. "I don't know how I will survive fourteen days with him."

"I thought you loved him?"

"Yes, I do. But he does not love me. All he ever does is shower me with gifts and presents."

"How long have you been together?"

"Too long. Thirty years."

"Any children?"

"A boy and a girl. Both have finished university and are married with their own families."

"You will be on your own then?"

"I want you to come with me."

"To Tobago?"

"He will never know."

"I have to go home."

"Are you married? Do you have a wife and children waiting for you?"

"No, I don't, but my ticket is to Grenada."

"I will buy you a new ticket."

"What about your husband?"

"I am booked in Coco Reef. I will book you into another room on another floor. Don't worry about my husband. He will spend only two hours with me during my stay."

"I don't know."

"Promise me you will at least think about it."

"I promise to think about it." I look into her sad, watery eyes. She holds my hand, squeezing it, and moves her body closer to mine. Her head falls on my shoulders as she continues to sob.

I stare at the roof of the plane. What did I have to lose? It's Thursday. I am not working on Friday. Monday and Tuesday are carnival celebrations in Grenada. I can miss that. There is a window of five or six days for me to make this woman happy.

What if her husband finds me? Suppose she is a maniac? Or somebody more sinister who preys upon the unsuspecting? My brain goes into overdrive.

But what is life without risks? Without experiment? Breaking new boundaries. The static from the in-flight recorder punctures my thoughts.

"Ladies and gentlemen, we are on our final approach into Tobago. Please store away your tables, return your seats to the upright position, put away all electronic items, and fasten your seatbelts. We should be on the ground within half an hour."

She looks into my eyes like a wounded rabbit. The tears are flowing down her cheeks. Gentle sobs transform into weeping.

Fear and doubt disappear from my thoughts. Here is a lonely woman. She needs companionship, and she has chosen me. How can I deny her?

"Tobago, here I come," I mumble.

THE END

A Bad Egg

Shanklin Chance feels the hot lead tear into his chest, forcing him to lose his grip on the balcony rail and begin his sixty-foot fall to the ground. It is as if someone planted a bomb in his spinal column, exploding and obliterating half of his back as the cluster of lead pellets exits.

Someone once told him that your entire life flashes before you during the moments before you die. He realizes this to be true as his eighteen years of life begins to stream to his brain from a huge projector in the sky.

At age four, Godson Chance, his father, introduces him to the surrounding bushes. Godson trains him to hunt iguana, manicou, armadillo, and monkey. His father tells him that the armadillo is the quickest and is difficult to catch when on the ground. The monkey is the smartest in trees. The alpha male spots the hunter from miles away and gathers his family to move. They move in unison away from the danger, deeper into the hinterland and safety.

Godson tells him the story of a female who held her baby to her chest, crying tears of sorrow so as to extract pity from the hunter.

Shanklin is eight when his father introduces him to the real action: breaking into houses and stealing the valuables. That day, they walk into the bushes without hunting. They dig wild yams, steal potatoes, and cut someone's bluggoe. They share the load. Godson carries the heavier bag.

Godson stops at the back of a house and points. "Tell me what you see?" he asks.

"A house."

"What else?"

"An orange house."

"More than that."

"Ah like it."

"What else do you see?"

"Windows."

"You are my son. From now on, windows will be your best friends. See that little one at the top? People always leave it open. That will be your secret weapon. Give me your bag and try it. Climb to the top using the waste pipe."

Shanklin hands his load to his father and walks to the base of the waste pipe. He climbs the pipe until he gets to the window. He looks to his father for further instruction.

Godson signals for him to push open the window. It opens in one try. Godson signals him to close the window and return to the ground.

On the ground, his father hugs him and returns his bag.

"That was easy. Next time you will enter, open the front door, and let me in."

Shanklin's body hits the ground hard. He cannot move. Blood hemorrhages from his back. His eyes scan the dark sky and fix on a distant satellite guiding him home. The movie of his truncated life continues to stream against the sky.

He is lying on his back on the mud flood of his parents' ply house. His mother, Gloria Chance, is scolding his father.

"I want to eat chicken today," she says. "Ah tired eating manicou."

"I have no money."

"Find it. I want chicken and rice. The children need milk."

"What you want me to do?"

"Ah don't care what you do."

"Well..."

Shanklin recoils as he hears the slap. Godson emerges from the single bedroom holding his jaw.

"Put your clothes on. Let's go," he says.

Shanklin gets up from the floor and puts on his clothes. He follows his father out of the door.

Shanklin follows Godson through the bushes. They run until they arrive at the back of the same house he climbed the day before. Shanklin climbs the waste pipes, opens the window in the bathroom, and climbs into the house. Once inside, he descends the staircase to the front door and opens it for Godson to enter.

Godson leads him through the house. Shanklin strays towards the kitchen, but his father steers him away. Godson shows him the typical spots where people leave their stuff. He points out the bedside drawers and the bedroom vanities: people always leave money there.

His father explains to him the order of priority. Hard cash first, light valuables such as jewelry and watches second, next cellphone and laptops. Then food.

They rob the house in less than ten minutes. Godson leads the way into the bushes.

Godson teaches him another lifelong lesson at that point. Never bring home the spoils, except the food. They stop at a cavity in the rocks. Godson removes a big stone to show a huge chasm. They pack their loot into the hole and walk home with the food.

Gloria is ranting when they get home. Godson ignores her. He goes to the kitchen to prepare the food they took from the house they raided.

Shanklin looks around at his six brothers as they eat. They were born fifteen months apart. The family sits in a circle on the floor of the kitchen. They eat from small bowls and drink artificial juice from plastic glasses. They devour the food.

He looks toward the sink to see Gloria leaning over it to eat, chatting with Godson. Shanklin sees she is pregnant again. She says she won't stop having children until she has a girl.

Shanklin gets up and walks outside to sit by himself and finish his meal. He loves being alone. It gives him time to think. He thinks of breaking into a house by himself. The spoils would be his—no sharing with his father. The way everyone looks at Godson when he brings home something—Shanklin would receive that look instead. He would get the praise. Shanklin to the rescue. Shanklin saves the day.

He rests his back against the ply house and looks around at the bushes. The thick dense green cradles him. It shelters his house and family from prying eyes and any form of wickedness.

Godson touches him on the shoulder, puncturing his thoughts. His father is carrying a plastic bag in his hand. He signals for Shanklin to follow him.

They carry the bag half a mile away to Betty John's place. They enter the house to see Betty breastfeeding a baby.

"Betty, ah bring you some food, girl." Godson says.

"Thanks Godson, I couldn't cook today. Ah was holding the baby all morning."

"But you must put her down sometimes."

"As soon as ah put her down she crying. Ah can't take the crying."

"You must let her cry. The priest say crying strengthens the lungs."

"The priest en ha no chile."

"Come boy, hold your sister." Godson beckons to Shanklin to take the baby.

Betty takes the baby off her breast and hands her to Shanklin.

Shanklin takes the baby and cradles her in his arms. He knows how to do this. He cradled his six brothers when they were this size. This is his first girl.

"Daddy, ah thought ah hear mummy say you couldn't make girl children?"

"Is she who can't make," Betty says.

"She says she going until she gets the girl," Shanklin says.

"As long as she doesn't take mine," Betty states.

"Me little sister sweet though," Shanklin says.

"How come she not crying on you?" Betty asks. "She knows she family. She like you."

Shanklin kisses the baby and carries her outside the house. Walking out of the door, he sees Godson approach Betty where she is sitting on the ground.

He continues to walk away from the house and carries the baby toward a piece of wood placed between the trees and sits there.

"I thought you had stopped that shit?" Detective Tim Roberts locks eyes with Godson.

Godson bows, looking at the ground.

The tall, lanky policeman stands to stare at the little man. "What made you start up again?"

Godson knows he vowed to stop. Under pressure from the police, he concentrated on his farming, hunting, and the irregular road-cleaning work. For many years, breaking into houses was but a distant memory.

"What happened?"

He hears the detective repeat the question. Educating him is not a choice. How could he tell Detective Roberts he is training Shanklin to take over the family business?

"I should lock you up."

Godson quivers at the prospects of prison. Two sentences to prison five years earlier convinced him to stop. Jail was not his favorite place. He doesn't want Shanklin there.

"Anyway, we know what you're doing and want you to stop now." The detective walks to the window and stares at the street. "You training your son. Let me warn you: the little boy's life is being destroyed."

Godson nods. He wonders how they found out Shanklin was there. They had their ways—so they always told him. "Anytime you break a place, we know," the policemen had told him.

"Don't know why I am wasting my time with you. You are a piece of shit." The detective turns away from the window. His eyes pierce Godson. "Get out of my blasted office."

Godson keeps his head bowed and slides out of the office.

Shanklin's head is throbbing with pain. His body aches and his legs quiver. The movie of his life continues to stream.

He is ten and breaking places on his own. Godson refuses to train him and go with him. Life is better without Godson—there are no restrictions. His father is always busy. Shanklin is not. He can break into places and spend as long as he wants.

One place he broke into he spent two days inside, eating, drinking, and sleeping. He loved the toilet. You pressed a button and water washed away the shit. At home, he sits over a hole in the latrine and everything stays there after you finish.

This independence gets him caught. He broke two houses that night. In the second one, he eats and falls asleep. A hand touches him. He wakes up to see a dark shadow over him. The shadow grabs him and carts him away.

Godson and Gloria sit across the desk from Detective Tim Roberts at the criminal investigations office.

"Talk," he sniggers at the couple.

"Ah dunno wha do the boy," Gloria says.

"Who do you expect to know?" the detective asks.

"Ah think they do him," Gloria says.

"Who you think do him?" Roberts asks.

"People doh like us," she says.

"Who do him?" The detective grins.

"Ah go find out," Gloria says.

"In the meantime, here is the position. Your son is distressing many people. He breaking places, eating people's food, destroying their valuables, and stealing their money. He is too young for prison. We don't have a juvenile detention center for people like him. What do you expect me to do with him?"

"I will cure him," Gloria says.

"You turn doctor now?" The detective grins.

"I can cure him," Gloria states.

Detective Roberts turns. "Bring him in," he shouts.

A female police officer walks into the room holding Shanklin by the arm.

"I am releasing him into your care. Handle him. Find a cure. Don't come back here. Next time we pick him up we will pass him through the court and process him like an adult."

The female officer hands over Shanklin.

Gloria and Godson stand to leave.

"On your way out, speak to the desk officer to pay his bill. Six thousand dollars."

"Whey we getting that?" Gloria asks.

"Ask him." The detective points to Shanklin.

The family moves to the next room to negotiate with the desk officer. They speak for a short while before leaving the police building.

Shanklin is sixteen and sitting in front of an obeah woman for the fourth time. Gloria is sitting off to one side, observing the ritual. This time is different. The obeah woman is white and dressed in a multicolored gown. Before, it was a black woman dressed in a white gown.

She does not raise her head. She is doing something on the floor with cards.

He sees the eerie shadows flickering against the wall as the light from the multi-colored candles dance. The smoke from the sticks of incense makes him drowsy.

At first, woman is reluctant to read. She agrees after she observes Shanklin and Gloria.

Later, she'll say that Shanklin was the most disturbed child she ever tried to help. She'll say she felt sorry for him.

The woman shuffles the cards, then spreads them on the floor, telling Shanklin to choose three cards.

Many years later, she'll tell people that "As soon as Shanklin picked out three cards, I saw I'd met a black soul from the bottom of hell. A horrible, evil young man who had no control over his actions."

The woman grabs witch's salt from floor nearby and throws it at Gloria, the mother of the evil.

Gloria sits there.

The white woman flicks over more cards, bows many times, and lifts her head to the heavens. She looks toward the heavens and continue to stare for a while. She lowers her gaze to look at the cards again. This time, she stands without extending her legs. The woman floats around the room. She looks into Gloria's eyes. Her hand extends to touch Gloria and retracts.

The white woman does not return to her original position on the floor. She settles instead on a raised platform a foot above her original position. She reaches for a bottle of water and sprinkles it on the floor in front of her, then sprinkles the rest on Shanklin. The water sizzles.

The woman recoils. "Get out," she says.

Shanklin rises to his feet.

"Both of you! Get out now," she screams. "He will die stealing. His blood will be on your hands."

Gloria and Shanklin run from the white woman's house.

Shanklin's movie twists. He leaves his body and floats over it, looking at himself lying on the ground. With his eyes shut, he sees himself floating. He remembers his first time in prison.

At seventeen, Shanklin is sentenced and sent to the main prison. They take him through the entry procedures and change him into prison drabs. An officer escorts him to his quarters. They tell him he will share the cell with two others.

The officer takes him to mix with the general population.

Several prisoners approach him but Shanklin speaks to no one. Dinner is at four p.m., after which everyone lines up, gets counted, and returns to the cells before six. He punches the wall of the cell in frustration.

A guard invites him to talk. They talk as they walk away from the cell into a darkened corner of the prison before Shanklin realizes that the guard has his hand around his waist and is caressing him. He stops walking and asks the guard to take him back to the cell.

Back at the cell, his two cellmates curl up on one bunk. They grin as he enters. He pushes his back against the wall and tries to settle. There are no bedsheets and no quilt, and he folds himself into a ball to keep warm.

He tries to read, but it's not his favorite pastime. With nothing to read, watch, nor discuss, he spends the next few weeks feeling cold, alone, and bored.

At the end of the week, he joins his two cellmates and huddles together with them as the third party in the lovers' triangle.

For the next year, Shanklin goes in and out of prison, spending between three and six months there at a time. Shanklin becomes a seasoned criminal, educated in prison habits and aggressive to the authorities.

The house he is falling from is three stories high. Earlier, he gained access through a window on the second floor. He cased the joint for four days. There was no movement. He believed it was empty.

The movie plays on. On the third floor, Shanklin makes his way up into the master bedroom. He rustles through the chest of drawers and scrambles among the jewelry on the shelves. He pauses as he hears a mechanical humming noise approaching the room.

Shanklin tiptoes out of the room onto the balcony, hiding behind the wall. The mechanical sound continues to approach, then stops. The house is quiet once more.

Shanklin slides away from the wall and peers into the open doorway to find the source of the noise. He sees the double barrel of a sawn-off shotgun mounted on a wheelchair and pointed at his chest.

The barrels of the weapon spit into his chest and he staggers backward.

He staggers into the wooden rails. Shanklin grabs at them. They collapse under his weight, and he loses his grip and begins the fall to the ground.

Shanklin's body twitches and jerks one last time, then goes still.

THE END

Pure Hope

It is a hot, bright Saturday afternoon in the summer of 2079 and Sasha and I are in the backyard of our home in South DeKalb, Atlanta, Georgia. We are barbecuing. The screen on my watch lights up as iRobot opens the door to our neighbors, Dick Stanton and his wife Jacqui. iRobot leads them through the house and into the garden to join us.

We hug and kiss and walk over to the sidebar.

"So, how was it?" I ask.

"Soothing," Dick says. "I thank you for the recommendation. We couldn't have chosen a better way to spend our honeymoon."

"Jacqui?" I look towards his wife.

"First class," she confirms, rubbing her stomach and curtsying to one side.

"I don't believe you, girl," Sasha states, grinning.

"Yes," Jacqui says, punching the air. "If it is a girl, we will call her Hope. If it is a boy, we will call him Hopeton."

"This trip blessed us," Dick says.

"Let us finish preparing the salad bar," Sasha says, signaling to Jacqui. They walk toward the kitchen.

Dick and I walk to the barbecue stands. We look on as Roomba flicks the pork on one stand and the chicken on the other.

"Dick, I want to know the full story," I say, checking my watch for an estimate of the remaining cooking time. "Start from the beginning."

"We enjoyed the royal treatment from day one, my brother," Dick says. "These were the best six weeks of my life."

"Most of all, you got the baby you guys were longing for," I say.

"Every day I pray for our baby. I ask that it remains well and sound. We want a healthy birth," Dick states.

"The baby will be great," I say. "You now have to think about school fees, books, and school uniforms."

"I am ready."

"Tell me about Hope."

"What a lovely place." Dick takes a thong from Roomba and turns the chicken on the grill. "We stayed at the Hope Island Beach Resort, an all-inclusive property. We had a fresh activity every day. No boring days."

"Glad you enjoyed it," I say. "Jacqui wondered about our recommendation."

"In the first week, we were a little skeptical," Dick says. "But the warmth and friendliness remained throughout our time. It never faded away, not for one moment."

"How was it outside the hotel?"

"That's the amazing part. As we traveled around the island, people treated us better."

"Did you go out?"

"There were trips available every day—we did them about twice per week."

"Where did you go?"

"We traveled to different sites on the island: the main city, forts, lakes, waterfalls, the tropical rainforest, heritage protected sites, other cities, museums, and cultural presentations."

"You guys have been everywhere."

"There are many choices. Tourists can do the city tours by walking guide, bus, train, or taxi. We booked our tours at the hotel with an agreed starting point. There is also an off-road tour you do with quads."

"How was the water?"

"Marvelous."

"Some days we sat on the beach and chill, sipping drinks covered with funny umbrellas. Other days we went scuba diving. One day we went underwater walking."

"How is the nightlife?"

"Parties every night, live bands. Sometimes we just had a quiet dinner."

"This is all so great. Too good to be true."

"I know." Dick removes the first batch of chicken from the grill, dips them in the sauce nearby, and lays them in a pan. "We kept looking for flaws and found none. Everyone we spoke to had offered glowing confirmation of our experience. No contradictions."

"What is the unemployment rate like?"

"No unemployment," Dick states. "The crime rate is zero. There was one murder last year. Two guys fighting about a woman. One stabs the other with a fishing knife."

"Wow." Roomba takes the first rack of pork ribs from the grill and dips it in my pork sauce before spreading it out in an aluminum foil pan.

"Yes. Wow."

Sasha and Jacqui emerge from the kitchen carrying two salad bowls. They set the bowls on the table. Dick and Jacqui grab beers while Sasha and I choose water.

We sit to eat. Roomba resumes control of the barbecue stands.

"Dick told me about your amazing holiday in Hope," I say, looking at Jacqui.

"Nothing short of amazing," she says.

"You know what that means." I bite into the tender pork, looking at Sasha. She returns the look and smiles.

"What?" Dick asks.

"We have to go see for ourselves," Sasha states. "You guys alone can't have all the fun."

"I agree," Jacqui says.

I ate and dreamt of a trip to Hope.

We can't sleep. Two excited little children promised a holiday by their parents. "I cannot control my enthusiasm," I say as we lie in bed, staring at the ceiling.

"I am worse than you," she says.

We'd been an inseparable team since the day we'd had our first conversation. I'd been doing anthropology work in US-occupied

Saudi Arabia and she'd been the US Army major in charge of my military escort. There'd been a major archeological find in the land of *Tema* and my team needed to finish its excavation.

I led the excavation group representing Harvard University as the senior authority in anthropology and the archeology of complex societies. I taught both disciplines at the university, besides teaching history.

Since the US occupation, we could not work without military escort. At first, she saw me as a liberated black man who stood against the military occupation and her job as a soldier. She had read my book *How the United States Undeveloped the Caribbean* and hated it.

At our first meet, I invited her to read my second book, *How the Caribbean Underdeveloped Itself*, and then she understood my position.

We hit it off like a refinery on fire. Six months later, we were married.

"So, we're going?" I ask.

"Yes, we're going," she confirms with a giggle.

We hug and continue to stare at the ceiling.

Sasha and I arrive in Pure Hope well into Sunday night. We were fortunate to get the last two seats on the supersonic shuttle that carried tourists from Atlanta to the island.

The airport is clean and well maintained. The officers scan our passports, pass our backpacks through the baggage scanner, and clear us for entry. Within twenty minutes of landing, we are at the taxi stand. On our way to the hotel, the taxi driver explains the full list of tours and activities available while on the island. We book him to pick us up the next morning.

We check into the hotel and receive a schedule of activities and list of places of interest. After checking into our rooms, we visit the restaurant for dinner, then head for bed.

The next morning, we are on the move. We take the tour from the hotel to the rainforest by taxi. At the rainforest, we potter around, pretending to be interested in the trees and vegetation around the crater lake.

One hour into the tour, we skip out on the driver. Sasha pretends she wants to pee and walks off into the forest, and I ask the driver to wait and follow her. The guard at the location waves to the driver and watches us go. We climb into the mountains for fifteen minutes before we hear them quarreling.

In the forest, we are one. Sasha's military training and my knowledge from my archeological climbs over the years means we're at home. Within an hour, we are on top of the mountain, enjoying the magnificent view of the island.

Sasha whips out her camera and takes pictures of the surroundings. I pull out my instruments and start to take measurements of a stone with recent inscriptions on it. I realize that people were here. The markings are as fresh as one week ago. Whoever wrote them spoke of topics in the news.

"Sasha," I called out. "There are people floating around here?"

"Yes," she says. "Check this out." She is holding the monitor on her camera toward me.

I walk over to her.

"Can you see it?" she points to a spot on the screen.

"There it is." On the screen is a man in the bushes with a heavy crossbow, squatting on his haunches and staring at us.

"What should we do?" She asks.

"Nothing." Options were racing through my mind. "Let him make the first move. We are in his place."

The man walks out of the bushes toward us, holding the crossbow in his right hand. "So, what brings you people off the beaten path?" His English is impeccable.

"Curiosity," I utter.

"You look like Yankees," he says.

"My grandfather is from this island," I say.

"That makes you a *belonger*," he announces. "We need you here. We need you to come back and join the revolution to take back our country."

"What is a *belonger*?"

"Anyone whose grandparents were born here is a *belonger*. A *belonger* has all rights and privileges."

"What is this revolution about?" I asked.

"This is a long story," the man says. "You will need to meet my leader, who will explain the revolution to you. I also cannot have you roaming around the place. You will get yourself killed. Come with us."

"Us?"

He puts his fingers between his lips and lets out a shrill cry. Three others emerge from the bushes to join him.

"They call me the Zagada," he chuckles.

"I am Vic and this is my wife Sasha," I say.

One man leads the way while we follow.

We did not walk for long. The men had stashed their electric quads in the bushes a quarter mile away from where they'd found us. The Zagada motions to Sasha to sit behind him while I ride with one of his men.

We travel for two miles. He raises his hand and we stop.

"Can you tell the difference?" he shouts.

"What difference?" I ask.

"The trees," Sasha says.

"You have a brilliant wife," the Zagada observes.

"Some of the trees are artificial," Sasha states.

I look closer at the trees and realize that many artificial ones are woven into the natural landscape. "Why?" I ask.

"Energy." The Zagada smiles. "All our energy comes from renewable sources. The leaves in the trees trap the energy from the sun, sending it down to the roots where our strands of fiber cables run to a series of batteries. We also use water turbines to provide back-up."

The quads move through the bushes following a solid, well-worn path. We arrive at a wall of trees that slides open before us as we approach. After entering, the wall closes behind us and we ride further into the belly of the mountain.

The Zagada leads us along a well-lit two-lane road through the rocks and into a wide underground opening. The Zagada and his men park the quads to one side and take us to a central main square, signaling for us to sit. Soon, the Zagada comes back with water and home-made sandwiches. We eat.

I look at Sasha. She looks relaxed. I am not afraid. From the beginning, the Zagada put us at ease. He has a disarming way.
A tall man with close-cropped hair and a graying beard exits a door at the other end of the square and walks towards us. I can tell he is a leader. He carries himself well in his military fatigues. He appears out of place. As he comes closer, I see he is a man better designed for urban life and a three-piece suit.

He puts out his hand. I shake the firm grip. He shakes Sasha's hand.

"They call me Iman," he says.

"I am—"

He waves his hand at me. "I know who you are," he says. "Follow me."

We follow him to a building on the compound. "You are Vic Thompson, the son of Victor Thompson, born in Atlanta Georgia in 2049. You majored in history and archeology at Harvard University. Received your PhD at twenty-five and you are now the youngest senior lecturer there. Your wife is Sasha Thompson, ex-US Special Forces, retired at the rank of major after serving in the Saudi Arabia war from 2069 to 2075. You met while in Saudi Arabia. Do you want me to go on?" Iman's eyes pierce into me like a laser.

"You got me," I concede.

"My full name is Ivan Mannford. They call me Iman for short. Both my father and grandfather were called Thomas Mannford. My grandfather, together with your grandfather, Victor Thompson, agreed to ship your old man off to the United States to protect our heritage.

"In 2019, people faced limited choices. Either you worked for the owners or you left the country. Those of us who stayed moved from the lucrative regions to the hinterland to live off the earth."

We enter an air-conditioned movie room and sit.

"My grandfather never spoke of you," I say.

"I think he did not want you to know," Iman states. "He didn't want you here. Can't say I blame him. Every day I ask myself what the hell am I doing here, and for who?"

"My friend told me this island is paradise," I say.

"Yes, paradise, but for who? Not for the *belongers.*"

"Our neighbor spent six weeks here with his wife. He told us this was the greatest place on Earth. We came to see for ourselves."

"Where did he stay?"

"Hope Island Beach Resort."

"That explains it. They take you where they want you to go. Where you get to see less than one percent of the story on this island.

I am sure he told you there was no crime, no unemployment, and food and drink in abundance in one big happy country."

"That's what they said," I confirm.

"Consider four sets of people. First, the hotel owners, who don't live here. Then the tourists who come and go. They enjoy the best treatment. Then there are the hotel workers, they work for pay. Then there is us. Those of us who fit none of the above categories."

"Are you considered unemployed?" I ask.

"No. To be unemployed, you must be in the city seeking employment."

"You're not?"

"Why would I? I don't do hotel beds. Do not serve tables at a restaurant. I am not a plumber," Iman stated, "nor an electrician. Nor do I clean swimming pools. At university, I studied financial modeling. There is no form of labor I can offer the owners."

"That makes you unemployed," I suggest.

"No, that makes me a societal drop out," he states. "I am of no use to society. People with academic knowledge are no longer required by this society."

"Are you serious?"

"You wrote about this in your analysis of these societies."

"Yes, I did." I hesitate. "My proposition was one possibility among several other variations that can arise if society takes a certain development path."

"They chose this path. Here we are today."

"How do you explain the lack of crime?" I ask.

"Crime has a strict definition. When a worker offends an owner or where an owner offends another owner, that is a crime," he explains. "When this occurs, they take the offender to the offender's country of origin for trial, punishment, and rehabilitation. This is why we have no prison."

"What happens when a worker offends another worker?" I ask.

"That is not as a crime."

"How is it dealt with?"

"That is a matter for management. It's handled in the workplace."

"Even in the case of murder?"

"Yes."

"What do the police do?"

"There is no police service. The owners pay security firms to safeguard their property."

"And the court system?"

"They scrapped the courts to save government spending."

"Health and education?"

"All taken care of by the owners for the workers."

"Help me to understand." I plan my thoughts. "A child who excels in school goes on to university in the United States and performs well—what becomes of this child?"

"There is no point in returning to Hope." Iman is blunt. "The natives who leave here don't return. Why would a qualified lawyer return to this island when there is no legal system?"

"So where do you and your community fit in?"

"There are several groups like us scattered around the island in small communities." Iman waves his hand. "They call us *drop-outs*, but we see ourselves as revolutionaries, knowing we shall overcome. We shall restore this country to the glory it once had. Our ancestors defeated slavery before our time. Now we face a new challenge. Slavery with pay."

Iman claps his hands to turn on the projector. The machine lights up and, after a brief establishment scene, a man comes onto the screen. I never knew him, but I recognize my great grandfather at once. He is standing in front of a huge crowd and speaking into a battery-operated loud hailer.

"Sisters and brothers, this is our last stand. We know we will die here today but we shall not be moved. We shall not be moved!" The crowd chants.

We shall not be.
We shall not be moved.
We shall not, we shall not be moved
We shall not, we shall not be moved
Just like a tree that's standing by the water side
We shall not be moved."

At that point, the police move in, armed with heavy tear gas canisters, sub-machine guns, and protective shields. While the crowd disperses, the police arrest many of them. My great grandfather is among those handcuffed, hustled into a police van, and driven away.

"We never saw him again. Later that night, they claimed he died in his cell from natural causes. The first autopsy showed nothing, supporting the natural causes theory. The second autopsy showed that he died from strangulation. Someone has applied pressure to his throat, fracturing the hyoid bone and making it impossible for him to breathe. The commissioner of police refused to cooperate. None of the officers on duty came forward. The director of public prosecutions refused to press charges. They held no coroner's inquest. The matter remains outstanding," Iman said.

I hear Sasha's sniffle and turn to look at her water-filled eyes.

"My father didn't tell me this."

"He did not want you to know. He wanted to protect you."

"From what?"

"The fire." I sense the laser drill into me and I shudder. "You did not come here by accident. This is divine intervention. God sent you here to help us overcome. Vic, you and Sasha must not go back to Atlanta."

Sasha comes over to hug me and lays her head on my shoulder. She is sobbing and trembling.

Sasha lifts her head from my shoulder to look me in the eye. She shakes her head. "Yes, we will stay."

THE END

The Twenty Second Bank

Selma Chopra places the two letters side by side on her conference table and closes her eyes. She leans back in her high-backed black leather manager's chair at the Twenty Second Bank. She knows she needs to decide. She doesn't know what.

For the next few minutes, she keeps her eyes shut as an unintelligible barrage of thoughts crashes through her mind. She opens her eyes to stare at the ceiling, remembering that she has to call the repairman to repaint the spot where he worked on a leak the week before. Leaning forward, she plants her elbows on the desk.

Selma flicks her hair away from her eyes and pumps four numbers into the phone followed by the number sign.

"Manager," the male voice slurs over the intercom.

"Please come to my office," she says.

"On my way," he replies.

Within minutes, her door opens and Assistant Manager Leon Job enters.

"Please sit down." She points to the chair across the conference table.

She pushes the two letters over to him. He reads the documents and frowns. His dreamy eyes rise to meet hers.

"Well?" she asks.

"Call the bank's attorney."

"What do I tell him?"

"He will tell you."

She presses the intercom. "Get Damion Green on the line for me," she says. "Tell him it's urgent."

Leon avoids her gaze as he waits for the attorney to come on the line.

The intercom crackles. "Mr. Green is on the line."

"Mr. Green, I am in my office with Leon, my assistant manager. I have you on speaker. We are looking at two documents we need your legal advice on. Can you give us a few minutes of your time?"

"Sure" Damion says.

"The first document is in your possession. It is the email from the office of Mikhail Cassis in St. Vincent. He wants us to move five million dollars from the account of Jon Davey at this bank in Grenada to an account held by the attorney Yasmin Hussain in Grenada. You will recall that I spoke to you about this transfer and you allowed it?"

"Sure."

"The second document is from the holder of the account, John Davey. John is requesting that we move the five million to an account held by him at the Co-operative Bank, Grenada."

"Seriously?"

"I will scan and email them to you."

"Please do."

"What do I do in the meantime?"

"Do nothing."

"Are you sure?"

"Yes, I am sure."

"How long will this take?"

"Relax. Leave it with me. That's why you pay me."

"So, I'll leave it in your hands."

"I will call you when I have something."

"Good."

"Bye."

She ends the call and looks into Leon's eyes. A chill runs through her body as his snakefish eyes return her gaze. She tries to read his feelings.

"That's it for me then?" he asks.

"What?"

"We will wait on the attorney."

"Yes... yes. You can go now."

"Enjoy the rest of the day."

"Thanks." She leans back in the chair to watch him slink out of her office.

The irritating sound of Skype on his computer causes Jon Davey to jump, just as it always did. He must remember to change the ringtone to something more soothing. Of course, then he might fail to answer it. He clicks on the mouse and Mikhail Cassis appears on the screen.

"I call to thank you." Cassis says.

"For what?"

"The money you sent us."

"What money?"

"The small matter of five million. I know that for people like you that is small money, so you may not remember transferring it to Yasmin's account."

"I did not send you nor Yasmin any money."

"She tells me it came from your account."

"Something is wrong."

"Not by me it's not."

"You need to return the money."

"Why should I?"

"It is not your money."

"It is now."

"I am going over to the bank."

"Try your luck."

Jon clicks on the mouse, zapping Cassis from the screen. He clicks on the intercom. His assistant answers.

"Bring me everything on the Twenty Second Bank."

The air conditioning is low at Yasmin Hussain's office, just as she likes it. Damion Green cowers into his jacket, sipping hot coffee and trying to keep warm. Yasmin shuffles the two documents Damion gave her, scrutinizing them for the fifth time.

The computer screen flickers and Mikhail Cassis joins them via Skype from his legal office in St. Vincent.

"I fail to see the problem." Cassis bellows from the computer speakers.

"The bank transferred the funds to Yasmin's account. Then they received a letter from the account holder, John Davey, requesting that the bank transfers the funds to his account at another bank in Grenada," Damion states.

"Who has possession of the funds right now?" Cassis asks.

"Yasmin."

"Don't you know possession is ninety-five percent ownership?" Cassis asks.

"Yes but…"

"There is no but. I have the money. It is his job to get it back from me. So, what is the problem?" Cassis states.

"The bank manager can't rest. She made a transfer from an account held by an individual without the written authorization of that individual."

"That is not our concern," Cassis states.

"What if the account holder goes to court?"

"Then that is a matter for you and your client. They pay you well to defend the bank. What is your opinion Yasmin?"

"You contracted me to be your local representative in this matter and I did that," Yasmin states.

"Do we owe Damion any money?"

"No. He received his cut for assisting us."

"So, what is he bitching about?"

"I am not bitching," Damion states. "I will have to develop a defense strategy."

"There you go my boy, that's the spirit," Cassis states. "Drive the BMW as a reminder of how you got it and you will come up with a solid defense."

"Do you feel better now Damion?" Yasmin asks.

"No. I still have no defense. This opinion does not help."

"Yasmin, I am out," Cassis says. "Let Damion earn his keep."

"Thank you for joining us Mikhail," Yasmin says.

Cassis disappears from the screen.

"Well." Yasmin looks at Damion.

"I will try to find something."

"You are on your own." Yasmin smirks.

"I realize." Damion finishes his coffee and leaves the office.

Jon Davey shifts his bulk in the visitor chair in Selma Chopra's office. He slings his leather side-bag across his body to rest it in his lap. Jon stokes his mustache with his left hand and flicks his silver Montblanc pen through the fingers of his right hand.

"Can I offer you a cup of coffee Mr. Davey?" Selma asks.

"No," he says.

Jon longs for a cup of coffee. At this time of the morning, he'd normally be kicking back and enjoying a smooth cup at his office. But he'd left the office to rush to the bank to confront the manager.

"I am having one made," she says.

The office attendant enters with a tray containing coffee, milk, and sugar. He avoids small talk.

"What gave you the right to move the money from my account?" he asks.

"Mr. Davey, I am sorry. I thought you people were all working together."

Jon hadn't expected that comment. Whatever gave the bank manager that idea? He is an accountant, the chief executive officer of his own organization, and the holder of the account at the bank. He knows all the lawyers, but that doesn't explain why she moved the funds from his account to an account held by the lawyers. Why does she think they're working together?

"Whatever gave you that idea?"

"I thought so."

"Why?"

"Damion told me you all operated together."

"Why didn't you ask me a question?"

"Damion Green said it was unnecessary."

He knows Damion Green: a little weasel who wormed his way around the court, trying to build a reputation for himself. This puzzles Jon further: the manager seeks advice from the bank's attorney and he instructs her to go ahead with an illegal transaction.

"He told you to go ahead with the transfer?"

"Yes."

Jon rises from his seat and leans closer to the bank manager. He trembles as he clenches the table. His face is shaking with rage. His voice is raspy and unsteady. "I must put you on notice. I will go to the DPP to press charges against your bank as a company and you in your personal capacity."

The bank manager recoils, rolling her chair away from the irate Jon. "Mr. Davey, If I were in your position, I would do the same."

"Expect to hear from the police."

"I can only express my regrets.

"I feel sorry for you." Jon grabs his leather side bag and storms out of the office.

"Give me a strong reason not to recall you to Trinidad," Ben Calderon states.

"I have none," Selma states.

"Then consider your stint in Grenada over."

Selma knows not to argue with Ben. He is a slow decision-maker. Once he concludes, he becomes resolute. As the CEO of the bank at the headquarters in Trinidad, he supervises the branches in the Caribbean.

He reiterates to her that he was the one who travelled through the region years ago to buy the regional branches at a time when the bank was on an acquisition binge, gobbling up every weak institution from Belize to the Bahamas. Ben's aim was to suction much-needed foreign exchange from the islands into Trinidad. He suspected that Trinidad was developing an insatiable appetite for foreign exchange which could only be satiated by external sources.

"I accept full responsibility," she says.

"You have one month's notice."

"Thank you for the opportunity to serve in a foreign country as a manager."

"When you get back, we will also talk about your retirement benefits."

"That will be fine."

She checks her position. At fifty-three, she is nearing retirement. She doesn't want to stay at the bank until she turns fifty-five. Her family in Trinidad worries her—they must not know that she's leaving the bank under suspicious circumstances. Her reputation as an honest, intelligent, and able banker must survive.

"Meanwhile, our legal department will work to clean up this mess."

"Why don't you give the man back his money?"

"No. That is not an option. The bank never admits culpability. We will fight him to the end. There is no way he can match our resources in court."

This does not sound good. She wants the matter to go away. Among Trinidadian Indians she is a hero: the strong Indian woman who manages a bank overseas and flies home sporadically. But she knows the managing director is unsympathetic. The only course of action he knows is litigation.

"But we are wrong."

"That's irrelevant."

"Sir, what is it about?"

"The bank. Do you expect the bank to agree to fraud? That will never happen. We will become the laughing stock of the industry. Are you that naïve Selma?"

"Yes sir. I am too old for this business."

"Yes."

"I will make arrangements to leave."

"Please do."

"Bye, sir."

Damion Green climbs out of bed, pulls on his boxers, and walks to the window of the room to gaze out. Through the window of the air-conditioned room he sees the expanse of the Le Phare Bleu restaurant sitting at the inlet of the bay. In the distance, he sees Cohen's island and two mega-yachts pulled up at the jetty.

He recalls working on that case. He negotiated the purchase of the island from its original owners and the later construction phase of the project. Despite the opposition and protests, he pulled the Frenchman through to finish his world-renowned resort and luxury holiday destination.

"Are you ready to leave?"

He turns away from to the window to see Darcy Mason sitting halfway up in bed, the top sheet covering his body.

"Not at all." Damion says. "I am stretching my legs."

"Stretch them here," Darcy says, patting a spot on the bed.

Damion walks back to the bed and sits facing Darcy.

"I am in no hurry to leave you baby," Damion says.

"You better be telling the truth. You're not trying to charm me like one of your clients are you?"

"I wouldn't dare. Remember, I had the greatest teacher." He smiles, kissing Darcy on the lips. He leans back and stares into Darcy's eyes. Darcy saved him in law school. At the University of the West Indies in Trinidad, Darcy helped him with his exams. Darcy is a quick learner and a patient teacher. He held his hands and guided him through the most difficult papers and frustrating times.

He kisses Darcy again and holds him in his arms for a while. "I love you," he whispers into his ear.

"I love you too," Darcy says.

At one point, halfway through the bachelor's degree program, Damion was unable to pay his rent and moved in with Darcy for several months. They were his best years at university. He got his meals on time, had spending money, and sailed through the rest of his exams.

"I will never forget how much you've helped me in life," Damion states.

"Ah, that's nothing."

Damion breaks away from the embrace and walks to the window. "I can't get enough of this view," he says.

Selma Chopra is ready to go home. The demands on her at the bank have been onerous. In the last month alone, she fired another 20 percent of her staff, bringing the total to 60 percent in the last two years.

Now, she'll get to be with her family. The constant travelling to Trinidad for short visits has been painful. The children are grown up, both girls at university, but her husband needs her most. He pretends to be fine, but she knows of his discomfort. The last time she'd left, he'd fought back the tears.

The knock on her door shatters her thoughts. She knows it's Leon. He has this habit of not using the phone extension, instead knocking on her door.

"Come in," she shouts.

Leon walks in, holding a brown envelope in his hand, and slouches into her visitor's chair.

What a lazy man, she thinks. He came to her six months ago. Head office hired him after she found herself without support staff.

"How are you coping?" he asks, placing the envelope on her desk.

"I am doing great."

"I am not."

"What is your concern?"

"Everything,"

She looks into his dreamy eyes. If she were to paint a mental picture of the man, she would use the darkest colors: dark grey, Spanish brown, mahogany, racing green, and dark lava. She questions his loyalty. He always bails out during a crisis.

"What's in the envelope?"

"My resignation."

"You've only been here six months?"

"Yes."

"Are you sure you do not want to give it a longer shot?"

"I have decided."

That is a color she forgot. Stone. "I am leaving too," she says. "I am being recalled to Trinidad. Most likely on retirement."

"I wish you all the best," he says.

"Thank you."

Leon stands and leaves the office.

Jon stares at Darcy as he ploughs through the file he handed over to him a short while ago. He gazes around the office while Darcy reads. A typical government office: stacks of paper scattered around the room, shelves of outdated books surrounding Darcy's back. It is amazing how government offices become dusty and quaint in such a short time. Government officers move into a new building and within months it takes on the identity of a "government office."

At his own office, Jon takes pleasure in clearing his desk every afternoon before going home. He has a sign on his desk saying, "A clean desk is the sign of a sick mind."

Jon watches Darcy flick another page, his eighteen-karat gold bracelet flickering in the old tungsten bulb hanging from the ceiling, and thinks how Darcy is out of place in this setting. On his left hand, the heavy Breitling gold watch matches the gold chain and name tag around his neck. The little diamond stud in his left ear and his low-cut hair.

Darcy lifts his head from the file and looks at Jon.

"What do you expect of me?" he asks.

"I expect justice. I want the bank, the bank manager, and the attorney who advised them prosecuted."

"That is not possible."

"What do you mean?"

"You have not presented me with a case I can go forward with."

"I don't understand—it is all there in the file."

"What you have here is a file containing paperwork."

"What do you need?"

"Do you have any witnesses?"

"People can testify."

"Do you have any evidence?"

"The manager admitted it."

"What if she changes her testimony? Which she will do under pressure."

"Take her written testimony now."

"The bank will send her home. She will not be available to give evidence in court"

"You are not prosecuting this case?"

Darcy looks away from Jon. He stares at the books on the wall, then lowers his eyes to the file on his desk. He hands the file back to Jon.

"You can keep these."

"What do you want me to do?"

"I have one suggestion. Try the civil route. File a claim in the civil division of the high court. That way you also get a shot at getting back your money."

Jon takes the file and leaves.

Jon grinds his teeth as he turns his Suzuki Grand Vitara into the wind-protected driveway. He drives along for fifty meters and stops just past the open gate.

"Boss not there."

Jon looks at the green and yellow parrot and smiles. "Timmy, I don't know what you get from lying."

"Boss not there."

"Anyway, good morning Timmy," Jon says and eases away from the entry point. In the distance, he hears Timmy shout, "Boss not flipping there."

Jon pulls into the yard and stays in his car. Within minutes, a Rottweiler and a Pit Bull Terrier circle the car, sniff at his tires, and walk away. Only then does he open his door and step out of the vehicle.

He climbs the short set of stairs and walks around the verandah to where Ulric Date is painting on canvas.

"Didn't Timmy tell you I am not home?" Ulric asks without looking.

"That lying parrot." Jon laughs. "You know he cursed me."

"He is testing his latest trick." Ulric places the brush in water, rests the small tin of paint on the stand, and turns. He opens his arms, inviting Jon into a bear hug. Jon obliges. "For a man who just lost five million dollars, you're looking good."

"You are worse than your blasted parrot," Jon says.

"Birds of a plumage," Ulric states.

"So you heard the story."

"Who didn't?"

"I am lost."

"You tried the DPP?"

"He was unperturbed."

"You know why."

"I heard the old talk," Jon states. "Didn't believe it."

"You better believe it." Ulric grins. "He is also one arrogant son of a bitch."

"What do I do?"

"Let us file the civil charges."

"Agreed."

Jon and Ulric walk into the registrar's office on Friday afternoon clutching a stack of papers. The registrar looks at her watch as the men step through the door. They hand over the stack of papers. She finds the affidavit's signature page and hands it to Jon. She administers the oath. Jon signs. She looks at her watch, then places her seal by his signature.

"I will have to date it as Monday," she says.

"Why?" Ulric asks

"It is one minute after four," she says, looking at her watch again.

"Mine says two minutes to four," Ulric says.

"I can only go by mine," she says. She signs, dates, and times the document. "This means that the document has to be dated Monday. It also means you have submitted your application late."

Jon and Ulric exchange glances. They finalize the remaining three copies of the document and leave the registrar's office.

Damion Green is driving along the Eastern Main Road when his car phone rings. He pulls aside to take the call. Darcy is on the line.

"I bring you good tidings my brother."

"Talk."

"Your troubles are no more."

"Ease the tension man."

"Just had a call from the registrar. You know the suckers filed late."

"Can't believe this."

"The judge will throw out his case."

"Celebration time, come on."

"Let's celebrate."

THE END

Queen Ivory

Ivory Zhu is standing outside Hunter Montero's office in downtown St. John, the capital of San Saba, and shouting into the building. She sees Hunter looking at her from the window on the second floor. Her voice bounces off the nearby buildings and reverberates through the streets of the city.

"I am a better woman than you," Ivory shouts.

Hunter sticks her middle finger up at Ivory and disappears from her lookout.

"Where are you going?" Ivory screams. "Bring your ass back here. You lazy bitch."

Hunter Montero walks to the telephone on her desk and pumps the numbers.

"One of your sluts is outside," she says.

"Hunter, you always with some shit," Theo Montero states. "Who is outside?"

"Your carnival queen. The one who says you can't leave her."

"Why would she be outside your office?"

"You should come see for yourself. She is ranting and raving outside."

"You don't expect me to come there."

"Do something."

"I will call Henry."

"I don't give a shit who you call. Get her out of my face."

Hunter returns to the window upright and composed.

Ivory is outside gesticulating. She flicks her hair extensions and sticks out her tongue, showing her stud. The diamond on her nose glistens in the sunlight.

"Yes, come back," she chides. "Ah not done with you yet." She looks around at the crowd gathering behind her. "I warming up for she ass," she tells them before turning back to Hunter's office.

"Theo tell me you can't cook, can't wash, and can't clean the house. He fed up wid you. You can't even mine dem two little children. He has to hire a maid for you." She turns to the crowd to whip up a chant. She removes her top to show her bra and faces the office. With a suggestive tap at the front of her leggings, she blows a kiss to Hunter. "You see wha he like. You can't test me."

Hunter signals for her to turn.

Ivory glimpses the policemen approaching from the side. She turns to see the crowd scatter while uniformed and plain-clothes police officers surround her.

Ivory kicks and screams, still shouting at Hunter, as they handcuff her and carry her away. Out of the corner of her eyes, she sees a tall and strong man nodding to the police. Ivory sees Hunter blow her a kiss before they toss her into the rear of a pickup truck. The truck drives off, tires screeching.

Hunter walks to her desk and flops into her chair sobbing. She pulls her starched collar and dabs at her eyes. The cotton makes her recoil. Her makeup stains the collar. Through her watery eyes, she presses the intercom.

"Tell the court I am unwell. I am seeking an adjournment for all matters down for today."

"Yes miss," her secretary states.

She pulls a tissue from the receptacle on her desk and dabs at her eyes. The array of pictures in front of her catches her eye. One is a portrait of her wedding day with Theo. Another shows her family: she and Theo at the rear and the two children standing in front.

She gazes around at her certificates on the wall. LLB with Honors from the Mona campus of the University of the West Indies, Jamaica. LLM with Honors from the University of Toronto. A specialization in Corporate and Intellectual Affairs from the Pace University of Law in New York.

On the wall next to her certificates hangs her robe, and next to it hangs her father's tattered robe. He gave it to her months before he succumbed to colon cancer. They had diagnosed his cancer nine months earlier. No program of chemotherapy, he told her. He'd lived a good life, he told her. She had to carry the baton, continue the work of the great Wilton Batson.

She dabs at her eyes with the tissue again, then pumps the numbers into the telephone.

"This is how you plan to deal with your marital problems?"

"What do you mean?"

"Send the police with Henry and his goons to take her away?"

"Not now. I am in a meeting."

"You listen. This is not the first time."

"We will talk about this when I get home."

"No. Leave the meeting. I can't tolerate this. Jamaica, Canada, New York… now here. Your hometown. When will it end?"

"I can't deal with your shit now." He slams the phone onto its cradle.

Hunter leans back in her chair and closes her eyes. Her memories of New York are recent; real and unforgettable. Theo was the ambassador of San Saba to the United States. They were at a party thrown by one of the other Caribbean countries. She was milling around chatting with the crowd when one of the wives observed that Theo was spending most of his night in the company of the lady ambassador from Venezuela.

She timed her intervention well. When he turned away from the lady to accept a drink from a passing waitress, she moved. I think you've had enough to drink. Let's go home, she said.

He looked at her.

She reached out to touch him. She was too slow. He slapped her hard with his left hand, balancing the drink in his right.

She shrieked and fell to the ground. He stepped over her and fled the scene. She took a taxi home.

Later that night, the police called her to come to the station. A patrol car had picked him up cruising in a red-light district four times over the alcohol limit. They refused to give her the details. The city will not press charges on the agreement that San Saba recalls him to the country.

The police looked at her blackened face. They asked her if she wanted to press charges for assault. She said no.

His father, Prime Minister Max Montero, recalled him to San Saba. She followed him home with the children.

Many years later, she learned why the police hadn't acted. It turned out that although he represented San Saba as a diplomat and had diplomatic immunity, Theo was an American citizen by birth.

She opens her eyes. Twenty years of dating, fifteen married, and still this guy's skeletons keep rolling out of the closet.

Theo slams the phone and looks across the desk at his father. Max Montero is aging and slowing. He spent most of the last week in bed, unable to walk. His swollen legs and aching hip hurt with the slightest movement. The doctors recommended a hip replacement, but Max declined. He told them that his friends who'd taken that course had either died or were alive and unable to have sex, which he considered being dead.

Max Montero was heading for his fifth term as prime minister of San Saba. He confided in Theo that he could not continue. He had not attended a meeting outside the island in the past six months. Travel was painful. He'd travelled to Cuba twice for medical treatment—both times by air ambulance.

"Hunter should know me by now. Women love me." Theo grins.

"This little Ivory is feisty," Max Montero states.

"She is a Caribbean queen."

"That does not give her the right to challenge your wife's power."

"I agree. What do I do now?"

"Same as you've been doing. Nothing. Maintain your silence, son."

"That's tough."

"Focus on your marriage."

"Dad, you sure about this? Why don't I give Hunter her divorce wish?"

"That's not on. Think about it. I handed over the Ministry of Finance to you last week. The party convention is in two weeks. You will become the party leader. Elections are due. I will step down. You are the next prime minister of San Saba. Losing your wife is not a choice. You can always kick her ass out after that. I hope you have a strong prenuptial."

"No, I don't."

"Then you have a problem."

"I was in love."

"So, what happened?"

"We grew apart as time went by."

"You mean your Montero genes overrode the love."

"Something like that."

"Anyway, focus on your political future," Max says.

"The party opposes me." Theo bows his head.

"Let me deal with that."

"I am just fed up of them."

"I know how you feel, but this is your life. This is my party. I built it—for you. Suppress your feelings."

"I appreciate that. It is this whole situation."

"That too will pass."

"Dad, I will follow your judgment."

"Trust me, son."

Prime Minister Max Montero picks up the phone and dials a number.

Donna Orlando answers the phone on the first ring. She recognizes the deep voice on the other end of the line. "Max, suppose they are listening to this call?"

"No one would dare bug my phone."

"What if my husband answered?"

"He knows about us. He is a smart chap."

"No need to rub it in."

"He knows he did not become the controller of customs on merit."

"Max, what do you want?"

"Theo has a problem. It will come before you. Make sure you handle it."

"Woman trouble again?"

"The Caribbean queen."

"When do I get to see you?"

"Soon baby, soon. I am resting just for you."

"I am here."

"See you."

Max turns to Theo. "You are all set, my son. Donna will take care of you."

"Dad, you sure about this?"

"You live and you learn, my son. You will soon understand."

"I don't."

"Let me tell you a story. The first time I came to office, I shifted around the permanent secretaries. A random shuffle. This lady comes crying. Because of the shuffle, she loses chairmanship of the board of directors of a para-state body. This causes her to lose

168

five hundred dollars. That five hundred dollars was going to keep her going for the month because her salary goes to pay her debts.

"Donna is a hopeless alcoholic and a freak. She wants to stay on the bench. I keep here there. Even if I don't want to. These women throw themselves into your hands. They force you to take control of their hopeless lives."

"You sure I am ready for this job?"

"You are. I was younger than you when I became prime minister. You grow with the job. It is a learning institution."

Ivory's eyes flutter open as the icy water hits her face. She scans the room. It's white. She sees the male nurse looking into her eyes. She tries to hit him but can't.

"Ivory, can you see me?" the nurse asks. "Blink your eyes if you see me."

She blinks.

"Great," he says. He taps her flabby hand to find a vein.

Ivory feels the medication flow through her body. "What is that for?"

"Some medication to calm you. A helper will take off your restraints. She will also help you get dressed for court. You appear before the magistrate today. You must behave when they remove the restraints, or they will put them back on."

She tries to move. He removes a strap from her hand.

She grabs him. "Before you go, I need sex."

"No. I will get fired."

"You don't want me?

"Yes. You are attractive, but I will lose my job."

"Where am I?"

"This is the special section of the Mt. Anon Mental Hospital."

"How long have I been here?"

"You've been here four days."

"Why?"

"You came here off the streets."

"Theo sent me here."

"I don't know."

"I want sex. Call Theo. Tell him to come and sex me."

"I can't do that."

"Did he come to look for me?"

"No."

"Don't go. Wait until the other person comes."

"Why? I have other patients to see."

She shivers. "I am feeling cold. I am lonely."

The nurse pulls a chair from the sidewall. "I will stay for a while."

"Can you loosen my other hand and my chest? I want to sit up. My throat hurts."

"That's forbidden"—the nurse pauses—"I will take a chance." He loosens the top restraints.

"Do you have cigarette?"

"But you are not a smoker?"

"I want to start."

"I have none."

Ivory sits up and surveys the room. Across the room, she sees a body being folded in a sheet and zipped into a body bag.

"What happened?"

"An inmate strangled him to death last night."

"While I was here?"

"Yes."

She feels the medication hit home. It relaxes her. "You can go now," she says. "I feel much better. I am ready for court."

Heavy showers are pouring on San Saba. Most of the town center floods. The main magistrates' court is leaking. Magistrate Donna Orlando moves her cases into the smaller traffic court.

The crowd cram into the little court and spill out on to the street. Protesters hold placards to support Ivory Zhu against the dictatorship of Max Montero and his son Theo.

"All rise for Her Worship Donna Orlando," the court officer bellows.

The crowd rises. Donna Orlando walks in and sits.

"Court is now in session," the officer states. "Please sit."

The magistrate calls the first matter for the morning. The State vs. Ivory Zhu.

Ivory, dressed in the same top and leggings she wore downtown four days ago, enters the courtroom. Without her hair extensions, her shaved head stresses her misery. The dark circles under her eyes spread on to her cheeks. Her eyes bulge out of her sallow face. The crowd gasps. An officer escorts her to the accused stand.

Magistrate Orlando whispers to the officer. He clears the court from the third row backward.

"Ivory Zhu, you are charged with using abusive language. How do you plead?" the magistrate asks.

"Not guilty," Ivory mumbles.

"Speak up!"

"I am not guilty," Ivory shouts.

"Prosecutor?"

"Your Worship, we ask that the defendant be returned to the Mt. Anon mental facility for further psychiatric evaluation."

The magistrate turns to the defendant. "What do you have to say?"

"Nothing."

"I sentence you to four months at Mt. Anon Mental Hospital for psychiatric evaluation."

Attorney-at-Law Rupert Mancini rises to his feet.

"Your Worship, I would like to assist the defendant in this matter," he says.

"You are not on record in this case, but the court will hear you."

"Your Worship, we all took an oath to assist the defenseless in their quest for justice, paid or unpaid. Retained or not. This young lady is the subject of abuse by a system protecting the rich and powerful.

"I cannot sit idly by while the state tramples on this young lady's rights. The dictator who runs this country and this court should be ashamed. At twenty-one, this young lady has already represented this country in many regional beauty contests. She is an international star. She is a queen. In her village, they call her Queen Ivory.

"Your Worship, have a look at the outpouring of support for this young lady outside of this court. Citizens of this nation have taken time off from their daily routines to come to this noble institution to influence the outcome of this hearing.

"I invite you to have a good look at Ivory. After only four days in the institution, she has already lost over twenty pounds. We have all heard the horror stories about this institution. To sentence her to spend more time there would make her crazy.

"An old man in my village told me he became crazy at the mental home when they shocked him three times and gave him tablets to swallow.

"I beg this court to release this young lady into the care of someone responsible in our society. She needs care and love, respect and understanding. Nurture her, don't discard her into a degrading environment."

"Sorry Counsel," the magistrate states. "I have already decided. Take her away. Now, the next matter on the list."

In her daze, Ivory hears the deep moans coming from the bench next to her. She hears the unintelligible words between the moans. She recognizes the voice.

"Tell me I am dreaming," she says.

"You are not dreaming," the nurse replies.

"Why is he here?"

"There is nowhere else to keep him."

"He goes to doctor overseas."

"The family is trying to fly him out. Until then, he is here. He is restrained and under watch."

"Will Theo be coming to see him?"

"I expect so."

"I will see my Theo." Ivory falls asleep.

THE END